I0760647

# THE WEST

## LAND OF OPPORTUNITY

## (A Collection)

**JOHNNY GUNN**

ILLUSTRATIONS BY
BARABASH SVIATOSLAV

# THE WEST

## LAND OF OPPORTUNITY

## (A Collection)

**JOHNNY GUNN**

**ILLUSTRATIONS BY
BARABASH SVIATOSLAV**

CONDOR PUBLISHING, INC.
Lincoln, Michigan

THE WEST: LAND OF OPPORTUNITY (A COLLECTION)

by Johnny Gunn

June 2024



*Cover and Illustrations by Barabash Sviatoslav

(All illustrations property of Condor Publishing, Inc.)

Library of Congress Control Number: 2024938743



ISBN-13: 978-1-931079-64-8 (hardback edition)

Condor Publishing, Inc.
PO Box 39
123 S. Barlow Road
Lincoln, MI 48742
www.condorpublishinginc.com

Printed in the United States of America

# TABLE OF CONTENTS

# INTRODUCTION

The West conjures ideas and thoughts in as many ways as there are people doing the conjuring. There are cowboys and Indians, miners and outlaws, ranchers and farmers, rivers and streams … just let your imagination go all in. Most of all, I think of the West as opportunity, then and now. Just as the pilgrims came to this continent looking for opportunity, their progeny moved farther and farther west.

Our first Western heroes were those men venturing into the Ohio Valley, men such as Daniel Boone. And we kept moving west, kept creating more heroes, until the continent was populated coast to coast. It is and was the people searching for opportunity that made the West what it is today. In these stories you'll find some really nice people, some really nasty people, and many simply looking for an opportunity to make their lives better.

Johnny Gunn

# TALKING TODD TAYLOR

Corporal Thaddeus (Todd) Taylor poured coffee for himself and two Crow scouts. It was September, it was cold, and it was night. Heavy Bow was a Crow, about twenty, and Henry Jordan, closer to thirty, was half Crow, half Black. Jordan's father had been a slave before running away and finding love and protection with the tribe. Thaddeus was just a white corporal following orders.

"Ah, I needed that coffee," Jordan said. "Gonna be a cold one tonight. The lieutenant should have been here by now."

It was getting late, but they wouldn't call it a night until their patrol caught up with them. They were part of the army chasing Chief Joseph and his band. The Crow scouts and the army had been following a well-defined trail left by the Nez Perce Indians in their race to the Canadian border.

"Reminds me of a night in the Black Hills just a few years ago," began Corporal Taylor continuing to chew on a cigar between sips of coffee. "We was chasing Elk Tooth and his renegades, and our patrol rode smack into the biggest mess of Sioux you've ever seen. Musta been a thousand of them screaming warriors."

"Gonna be a long story, Taylor?" asked Jordan, and then he scrunched down into his bedroll, fighting off a combination of cold and another long yarn from the corporal. "Wake me when it's over."

It was Captain Johnson who gave the corporal the moniker Talking Todd Taylor. Taylor had been in the army since the day he turned sixteen, about fifteen years ago, and many were sure he had never stopped talking that entire time. Some of his tall tales were epic, hours long. His penchant was speaking around campfires, such as this one tonight.

"Have you ever told the truth?" chuckled Jordan.

Unable to sleep, the scout sucked on his pipe and propped himself up on an elbow, getting ready to endure another incredible yarn.

"Ain't never lied a day in my life," said Taylor, and huffed himself up and chewed hard on that old cigar butt. "No, sir, I never felt it necessary to make up fables of what this fine army is able to do. Why, when I rode with Colonel Buster Whalen, way back when, there weren't a red renegade that wasn't skeered, hearin' we was comin'."

The cold was intense, the night couldn't get any darker, and Taylor was primed.

"I led a patrol into a ravine, chasing six renegades, and they rode up to a main force and turned back on us. Why, what else could troopers like the ones I was leading do but hunker down and fight? They was ten of us and fifty or more of them. My rifle barrel got so hot I was able to light my cigar on the receiver end."

Taylor took a swig of coffee and chewed harder on his cigar.

"Four of my men died in glorious combat that day, boys. But, we routed those redskins, captured a head chief, we did, and got commendations all around. Why, listen here, old Colonel Whalen give out the commendations hisself, he did."

"Ain't heard about that battle," Jordan said. "Did that battle have a name, Corporal?"

"Shore did. Battle of Coyote Canyon. Back in 1860 something. Cain't remember the exact dates. There were so many battles back then. Constant combat, it was."

The corporal continued as he threw a chunk of wood on the fire.

"There was another fight," resumed Taylor, "and our little squad got caught in the open prairie by a bunch of Cheyenne, screamin' for my scalp. I had a reputation back in those days." The corporal paused, took a sip of coffee, bit off another chunk of that old butt, and hesitated. "They was forty of 'em and just the ten of us. We were laid out in prairie grass behind our ponies, firing shot after shot after shot."

"You don't say," smirked Jordan.

"Why, bless me for telling it like it was, Mr. Jordan. Only two survived our wonderful marksmanship. Then we marched those two back to the fort, makin' them drag a travoise with our wounded lieutenant on board. Oh, it was magnificent combat."

Taylor told another yarn or two before the patrol finally rode in. The unit found them by following the fire Taylor's men kept burning.

"Thanks for the fire, Corporal," said Lieutenant Samples. "Back in the rocks like you are, wouldn't have found you without it."

Lieutenant Broderick Samples was on his first assignment west after graduation from the Academy.

"You got here just in time, Lieutenant!" Heavy Bow's rumbling bass voice spoke out of the darkness. “Our fine corporal is telling of the times he rode with Colonel Whalen. Have you ever heard of that man?”

“Colonel Buster Whalen?” asked Samples, walking to the fire and pouring a cup of coffee. “I grew up at Camp Johnson down in West Texas. Colonel Whalen was named superintendent of the West Texas Department and given his first star there. He was a fine cavalryman if there ever was one.”

The lieutenant looked his corporal up and down, swilled some coffee, and spat it out.

“You rode with Buster Whalen, Corporal? That makes you special in my book. Whalen’s reputation extends all the way back to West Point; it does.”

“Thank you, sir,” Taylor said. “Why, I was with Colonel Whalen in Texas. We fought the Cheyenne on a weekly basis in those days. I can tell some hair-raisin’ stories about them times. We had Quanah Parker trapped up once, but he got away. Me and Colonel Whalen almost had the man, but I took an arrow and we had to stop.”

“You chased Chief Parker, and now you’re chasing Chief Joseph? Amazing,” the young lieutenant said.

“Yeah, amazing,” Heavy Bow grunted. “Next, he’ll be telling us he was with Fetterman.”

"No, Heavy Bow," replied Taylor, "we missed that one. It was at Coyote Canyon where me and Colonel Buster Whalen made our mark. Fought them red warriors for two days solid, back to back. Got down to hand-to-hand, and I killed the last one just as he was about to slit the colonel's throat."

"I'd sure like to meet this Colonel Whalen someday," Henry Jordan said. "Compare his stories to yours."

"He's around somewhere, Mr. Jordan," Lieutenant Sample said. "He's a major general now, though. We'll stay on Joseph's trail tomorrow, Corporal, then head to Clapsock Village to resupply. You and the scouts leave before sunrise. He's making for the Canadian border, and we should be able to cut him off soon."

"I'll finish the story about Coyote Canyon in Clapsock Village, Lieutenant," said Taylor.

The young lieutenant looked hopeful while Heavy Bow and Henry Jordan groaned quietly. The lieutenant was thrilled to be in the West, fighting Indians, although, except for his scouts, he hadn't even seen one. He wanted to hear the stories but wondered if there was any truth to them.

*Well, he did know about General Whalen,* thought the lieutenant. *He knew about the Coyote Canyon affair. Maybe some of the stories are real.*

Lying down, the lieutenant slept well that night. The next morning, Corporal Taylor and his scouts were four hours out when they ran into a large army formation moving toward Clapsock Village. Taylor and two scouts advanced to speak to the officer in charge. The corporal saluted.

"Where are you headed, Colonel Fogarty?" asked Taylor.

"Clapsock Village," replied the officer. "Chief Joseph just gave it up. Says he'll fight no more, forever. You with Lieutenant Sample's patrol?"

"Yes, sir."

"Go back and get the patrol and ride for the village. Our job is over, Corporal."

"Yes sir, as you order, sir!" replied Corporal Taylor.

* * *

The group of three found Lieutenant Sample an hour or so behind them, and the scout, Heavy Bow, laid out the trail for Clapsock Village.

"Surrendered, did he?" said Lieutenant Sample. "He was a fine warrior, always thinking of his people. A good leader. Maybe we'll get to meet him."

"You have an interesting outlook, Lieutenant," replied Corporal Taylor. "Ain't the way I would have called it. Why, one time, down in Texas, all we wanted to do was kill old Chief Parker. This Chief Joseph is responsible for a lot of soldiers dying, too."

"Times are changing, Corporal," said the lieutenant. "There'll always be a need for a strong army, but we gotta learn to choose our enemies with a little more thought involved. How long to Clapsock, Heavy Bow?"

"It'll be dark long before we get there," grunted Heavy Bow. "Depends on the corporal's stories."

Lieutenant Sample chuckled but wondered again about many of the tall tales Taylor told. How could this one man have been in so many major battles? Or ride with so many real heroic officers and remain an unknown corporal of scouts? The lieutenant wondered if maybe this Talking Todd Taylor was a drunkard when not on patrol.

"You'll have to tell me about some of these battles and actions you were in with General Whalen, Corporal," said the lieutenant. "That is, when we get to Clapsock Village. I've studied many of the general's campaigns while at the Academy. Might be interesting to get your take on some of them."

"Be glad to, sir. Best fightin' officer I ever served with."

* * *

There wasn't much to the village of Clapsock—just a thrown-together hardware and general merchandise outlet, a couple of tent saloons, one or two not yet completed wooden buildings, and a lot more tents. There was gold in the Clapsock Creek and its tributaries, good grass on the northern plains, and frigid temperatures driven colder by wind. Lieutenant Sample led the small patrol into the army garrison grounds and made his way to the headquarters tent.

"You were almost there, Lieutenant," said the colonel. "Your scouts had a good bead on Chief Joseph. Good job. Taylor give you any trouble?"

"No, sir. He and the scouts did a fine job. What kind of trouble, sir?"

"He gets to telling those wild yarns of his and forgets what his job is," replied Colonel Fogarty.

Officer Emory J. Fogarty had come west immediately after the War Between the States as a major. He made a good name, getting various tribes and groups onto reservations. Chief Joseph's surrender would add to that reputation.

"A trainload of generals is expected in the morning, Lieutenant," said Colonel Fogarty. "I want you and all the officers in your finest and on the parade grounds to welcome them. We'll do a full parade and review of the troops at that time."

Lieutenant Sample left to spread the word. He wanted to get his platoon squared away and ready and then find a cold beer. This was as close to civilization as he had been in several weeks. It was dark, cold, and windy as he walked out of the encampment. Wet snow was falling, and he dreaded the formation come morning.

One of the tent saloons was filled with civilians while the other was mostly soldiers. He picked that one for his beer. It had a dirt floor, just planks on barrels for a bar, and oil lamps for lighting. There was a lively group of soldiers off at a separate table. Sample noted that the man leading the festivities was none other than Corporal Todd Taylor.

"Talking Todd must be telling wild and vivid stories," Sample muttered.

The lieutenant wanted to join and listen, but he knew he would not be welcomed as an officer. The barman was an old and grimy man. He limped on a wooden leg and growled more than spoke.

"Well, Lootenant, you gonna drink or just stand there?"

Trail dirty, tired, and cold, Sample jumped at the comment.

"Cold beer, please."

He realized he was paying more attention to Taylor than to getting served.

"That man sure has a lot of stories to tell," commented the young officer.

"Lies," the barman said. "They be lies, or I'm not Irish. Man ain't never seen real combat. Shoulda' been with us at Gettysburg. Then he'd a had something to tell about. Now, about that beer. We got beer, but if you want it cold, that's outside."

The barman coughed hard, and that was as close to a laugh as he could conjure.

"I don't know," Samples said. "Some of those stories Taylor tells, I've heard myself from General Whalen."

"I ain't in a mood to call you a liar, Lootenant. But Talking Todd Taylor? He is a liar."

Disgusted, the bartender limped down the bar, scowling, cussing, and coughing.

Sample enjoyed his almost-cold beer while he listened to a couple of tall tales from Taylor's table. The officer watched it get even more lively as more whiskey was poured. Sample headed back to his tent.

"That's sure to end in fighting before too long," chuckled the lieutenant out loud. "This'd be a good night to be an enlisted man."

* * *

The parade ground was a muddy quagmire at sunrise. The rain and snow mix continued to fall, and the wind was far beyond gale force. Lieutenant Broderick Sample led his platoon into forming a welcoming pageantry.

"What's with the limp, Corporal Taylor?" asked officer Sample.

"Took a nasty fall, sir," replied the corporal.

Sample heard some soft laughter in the formation.

"Fall, Corporal?" asked the officer.

"A couple of men didn't like some of his stories," one of the troopers opined. "Took offense, called him a liar, and all hades broke loose."

"I don't lie, sir," Taylor said.

Bugles sounded, the formations came to attention and a cadre of riders came through the gates. Flags were flying, followed by four generals in all their splendid finery. A full guard company rode behind them. There was a gathering in the middle of the parade ground. Everyone dismounted, and led by Colonel Fogarty, the generals began their review of the troops.

Up one line of rigidly at-attention troops and down the next, the officers reviewed the company. The generals' shiny boots stepped through the slop and mud.

"That's Major General Whalen," Lieutenant Sample muttered under his breath, watching as the brass moved slowly toward his platoon. "My Gosh, I might learn something here."

Talking Todd Taylor had his squad lined evenly as the generals began to walk through. One stopped instantly, right in front of Taylor.

"Corporal Taylor, is it?" said the officer, staring at the trooper's face.

"Yes, sir, General, it is I. Have you been well, sir?"

The comment brought the other officers up short, and they all glared at the enlisted man. Who is this corporal to talk that way to a general officer?

"Ha, it is you!" General Whalen howled with joy. "General Howard, sir, this is the man who saved my life twice in terrible battles we fought. Once, it was at Coyote Canyon, as I recall. A Cheyenne had me on my back and was about to slit my throat when Corporal Taylor here killed him dead. It's good to see you, Taylor. Good to see you. Let's see if we can get together and reminisce, eh?"

Taylor was ramrod stiff as General Whalen led the group on down the formation, but he simply couldn't hold his smile in check. Lieutenant Sample's mouth hung open for a moment.

When the formation was dismissed, hundreds of dollars changed hands, some between line officers, some between non-coms, and some between enlisted personnel. The obligatory paying off on bets on whether the stories were bunk or not. Taylor drank free at the soldier's saloon that night, and those who believed his tales enjoyed their pockets being full of greenbacks. Lieutenant Sample had supper in the same tent as General Whalen, but he never had a chance to talk with the officer. Whalen spent most of the night telling tall tales and war stories about his time with Talking Todd Taylor.

POST OFFICE
HOTEL

# GROWING COWS OUT OF THE WIND

It's the wind that finally knocks you down for the count, not winter's blizzards, not spring floods, not even the late frosts that kill the bunkhouse garden. No, sir, it's the wind—incessant, cold, warm, putrid, hot, and scalding—sand blown into every crevice and wrinkle in or on the body.

Nick Jenkins had been working the Bar JC ranges for more than a decade when he cantered into the corral one afternoon, tied off his paint gelding, pulled his gear from the bunkhouse, and called it quits.

It was an hour's ride into the little village that grew up around the big ranches in the area. Nick rode right up to the saloon, hitched his horse, and headed inside.

"Beer, cold," he said, speaking to anyone who might have been listening. "I weigh about a hundred and eighty, and eighty of that is the sand I ate chousin' them steers today. Ain't doin' it no more."

His horse taken care of, a hot bath and a big steak followed. It gentled Nick out some, and he was back in the saloon.

"Hank'll bring my final pay here, Tiny. Hold it for me, will you?"

"Sure, Nick. You really giving up buckarooing?"

"I'm just gonna look for a place where they grow cows out of the wind. My ears are half the size of yours, Tiny. Been sandblasted to shreds. My nose hurts all the time. I wash a beach full of sand out of my eyes every night and find more in the morning. Ain't never took my boots off that I didn't shake out a pound of dirt blowed into 'em. Yup, gonna find a place where they grow cows, and there ain't no wind."

It was five o'clock in the morning when a bangin' and crashin' outside his room woke old Nick from a sound sleep. He fumbled his way to the window only to find the hotel sign spread across the dusty street in several pieces, some still being blown about by a gale howling through the village.

"It just figures," he said, struggling into his pants and boots. Shirt tucked in, sand washed from his eyes, he sauntered downstairs for breakfast. "I'd be out in that blowin' tempest if I was still a cowboy," he mumbled through a gentle smile.

Downstairs, he ordered a platter of hot cakes, eggs, and ham from Tiny's wife, Hilda. He was on his second cup of coffee when his friend Hank, the cow boss, came rattling into the cafe, spur rowels singing against hardwood.

"Fences down everywhere, Nick! Need you! Now, boy, now!"

"But I quit, remember?"

"That was yesterday. Grab your gear, and let's go."

There was no argument that stood up to Hank's insistence, and Nick got his gear, slipped into his batwing chaps, tied on his spurs, walked with his head down to the horse corrals out back, threw a loop over his paint, and sighed, ever so gently.

"Hoss, I need someplace where they grow cows out of the wind."

The words were hardly out of his mouth when he spotted his boss, Hank, loping down the street past the mangled hotel sign, trying to catch his sombrero.

Territorial prison
2 miles

# HE KNOWS HORSES

The two men were standing at tall gates with high fencing stretched out on either side. One was wearing a holstered revolver and carrying a double-barreled shotgun, while the other was wearing dirty pants, a shirt, worn-out boots, and a pitiful sombrero.

"You done your time, Pollack, you're free. Here's two dollars, and good luck."

"Hope I never see you again, Tanker. Those were the worst three years of my life," said the ex-prisoner. He walked over to a waiting stagecoach and was about to throw his kit up to the driver.

"It's three dollars to town. In advance!" snarled the driver.

"Forget it," said the former prisoner, Ryan Pollack. He tossed his kit over his shoulder and began the five-mile walk to Spencerville. "Three long years wasted, and I've got a whole two dollars in my pocket. Well, it isn't the first time I've started over," he muttered to himself, kicking up some dust with his boot toe. "I'm Ryan Pollack, free man, and I ain't never goin' back to prison."

Pollack was seventeen when he left his home in New York City and headed for the gold fields of California.

*That was my dream,* he was thinking, as he marched toward civilization. *Never got to California and never have seen a real piece of gold, except them coins. But man, have I had some times,* he thought as a smile ached its way across a face that hadn't smiled in a long time. *That was fifteen years ago, I think, and I never got past Wyoming, and look at me now. Son of a gun, but I'm one big mess.*

Out west Ryan was taught bronco busting. First, he learned the cowboy way, which is pretty tough on the critters and men. Then an old Spanish vaquero took him in tow and taught him the real way of horsemanship.

*I know this is ranch country; I've seen the herds come by, so maybe there's a chance for me yet. No more Mr. Big Shot, know-it-all, Ryan Pollack. From now on, I'm Ryan Pollack, a man who works horses.*

The five-mile walk from prison to town brought so many memories back to Pollack, memories he hadn't had the inclination to think about. He picked up a rock, leaned back, and hurled that stone at a wildflower alongside the trail.

"Well, I'll be. I haven't throwed a rock in ten years, and look at that. I hit that posy."

It shouldn't take a man more than two hours to make that walk into Spencerville, but this was Pollack's first taste of freedom in three years. With flowers and grasses all along the trail, birds flying up, and rabbits scampering off, daydreams began dancing through his head, and the walk took longer. The trail crossed a small stream, and Pollack stopped to splash cold water on his face.

"Man, that felt good," he said as he knelt down and cupped a cold drink. He splashed some more water on his face, dumped the crumpled old sombrero in the water, and put it back on. "I'm gonna need to camp tonight. Two lousy dollars ain't gonna get me much in Spencerville."

He got back on the trail.

*Where in heaven's name did I go wrong? How did I end up in prison? I never stole nothing from no one, never tried to do a man wrong, but sure as all get out, I did kill that fellow up on the Yellowstone. Surely, I did.*

His mood was changing; he could feel it, the anger returning, the problems that led to the fight, the instinct to win, and the know-it-all attitude that may have brought on the problem.

*I was working for José Maldonado,* thought Ryan. *Training and breaking horses for his remuda, living the best life a man can live. José was a good man, and we got along well. We talked about not having slept in a bed and about not having a meal inside a building in a year. We knew it simply couldn't get better. Maldonado took me as a boy under his wing, teaching me Spanish, the way of a vaquero, and the Spanish way with horses. I had never even seen a hackamore till I tangled up with that crazy dude. I didn't know what a vaquero was; I didn't even know you could throw a loop as far as that man could.*

"That was where the problem started," he mumbled. "I had learned the vaquero way, had become an excellent rider. I was proud that I could work with the meanest caballos on the line, and have them wanting to be under my control and not fighting it. But, I never could learn to braid a reata."

*Me and old José,* thought Ryan. *Good times and I screwed it up. And dumb old Caleb Redstone had to come into our lives.*

Pollack was fighting off the memories, but he also knew he had to get it out of his head.

*That Caleb just got under my skin, and José warned me more than once, to stay away from him. Couldn't do that, not me. Just rile that boy and get it over with. Never did listen. I called him an ignorant pig one time, and we busted each other's faces pretty good, but the problem came when he chased after me with a knife. I surely did kill that man.*

Pollack could see Spencerville as he topped a rise in the trail and looked around for a place to spend the night. There was a nice stand of cottonwood trees about a quarter mile outside the village. It was well away from any of the trails leading in or out, and he walked over and set about making camp. He spread open his kit.

"Well, look at that," said Ryan, opening his pack. "They actually gave my knife back. I was worried about that and my flint striker."

He picked up a couple of nice-sized throwing rocks and ventured to the meadow. Ryan came back shortly with a long-legged, flop-eared, skinny-as-a-fence-rail jackrabbit.

"Beats the heck out of prison slop."

He watched the stars slowly appear, put another couple of sticks on the fire, and finished cooking and eating the rabbit. He doused the fire and pulled a blanket around his shoulders.

"First night as a free man, and I'm sleeping under the stars, eating wild meat, and feel like the luckiest guy in the world," he said out loud.

Since his release, he tried to push it out of his mind, but if he didn't come up with some way of making money, it would be a long, tough winter. He needed to get a job in town or at a ranch as quick as possible.

In the morning, he had a drink of cold water for breakfast, found they hadn't given his razor back and couldn't shave.

"Wonder what Spencerville is like? Awful close to that prison. Suppose I look like I just got out. This is embarrassing."

He scrunched the old sombrero down on his head and went into town. Ryan walked down the main street of the little village. He noticed there were two saloons across from each other, a hotel with a barber/dentist shop attached, and various other businesses.

*Looks like a busy place,* he thought

Ryan spotted the livery stable. The smithy, big and brawny, was firing up his forge. He started his fire with wood, followed by buckets of coal.

"Mornin'."

"Boy, you look like a bad piece of something," observed the blacksmith. "You just get out of that hell hole down the road?"

"That obvious? Yep, three hard years, but I promised the world, I ain't ever goin' back. Before I got in trouble, I was a good man with a horse; right now, I could use a job. You need a hand?"

On the walk into town, Pollack had decided the best bet would be straightforward, don't lie, tell it like it is.

"We'll talk horses later," said the blacksmith. "You any good with a pitchfork and shovel? I hate cleanin' stalls. Got a stable needs cleanin', two corrals, and about ten horses to feed. Give you a dollar a day and a place to sleep if you want it. No smokin' in the barn. If you steal somethin', I'll shoot you dead," said the blacksmith, and there wasn't a smile attached to that comment.

"Ain't never stole nothin' in my life, Smithy, and I think you'll find I'm a-workin' fool."

"You ate yet?"

"Nope. Cold camped outside town."

"Bring your gear in and put it in the back over yonder, and we'll go have breakfast and talk some. Name's Henry, Henry Workman. Horseman, huh? We'll see."

Pollack put his kit in the livery.

*A dollar a day and a place to sleep,* thought Ryan, *and I haven't been in town for an hour. Now, for sure, I'm a free man.*

Ryan and Workman walked to the hotel and found seats in the restaurant.

"What makes you think you're a horseman, Pollack?"

"On the Spanish and Mexican ranches," replied Ryan, "there are charros, cowboys, and vaqueros, the men who train and work ranch horses. I worked with a Spanish vaquero for more than five years. He braided his own reatas and could throw a loop fifty feet. There is a calmness to the vaquero methods, and I learned much from my friend."

"I've heard of such things." Workman nodded as the two dove into great chunks of beef covered in gravy and platters of biscuits to soak it all up. "Man works hard; man needs to eat well," he said, smiling for the first time that morning.

"Ten horses is a pretty full stable," said Ryan. "You always booked up like that?"

"Seems like it," replied Workman. "You'll earn your keep, believe me, and you should have enough time to work with a horse or two. I do want to see you ride."

* * *

What with having to buy his main meal, it took Pollack more than a week to have enough money to purchase a new pair of boots and a shirt.

"New pants just gonna have to wait a spell."

He got up at sunrise, made a pot of coffee, ate some hard tack, and spent several hours feeding horses and cleaning stalls and corrals.

"You used to do all this yourself?" asked Ryan.

"Heck no, boy. I hate that kind of work. Stomp out the little problems, yup, I'd do that, but I'd grab anybody handy to do the corrals and stalls."

"You run a good business, Henry Workman," said Ryan.

The two men became more than boss and hand almost from the moment they met, and Henry was quick to help out his new man.

"I got a deal on a colt yesterday," said the blacksmith.

"Yeah, I met him this morning. One fine-looking horse, Henry. Good conformation, bright eyes, and curious. It's a good sign if they're curious."

Pollack told the blacksmith that if the horse had any training at all, it was brutal, and the young stud shied away from contact. But he also thought that the horse would respond to good handling.

"You want to bring him up to speed?" asked the blacksmith. "It ain't in me to do that kind of work. I love a good horse as long as someone else does the training." He gave out with a belly laugh. "Yep, that's my way. You feed 'em, you clean up after 'em, you train 'em, and I'll ride 'em."

Both men laughed.

"I'll do my best to make him one fine horse, Henry."

Pollack walked off toward the corral, thinking what a huge change had come into his life in such a short amount of time.

"I screwed up my life, old pal," he mumbled to the young horse, "and I've paid for it. You've had a hard start on yours, and I'm gonna try to make up for that."

Pollack walked slowly into the pen with nothing in his hands. Old José had taught him this trick about not scaring a horse. He wiped his face with his kerchief, took his sombrero off, ran his fingers through his hair, and just ambled over to one of the fence rails and leaned up against it. He looked around the corral and ignored the colt. The young stud horse stood almost fifteen hands. Ryan watched as curiosity got the better of the animal.

"Probably about three years old, I'd say," he mumbled and watched for another few minutes.

Just about that time, the horse decided to check him out. Pollack moved off the rail and ambled around the corral some. The man followed the fence line. He avoided the animal, careful not to walk towards it. He stopped, leaned against the rails, and kicked some dust with his new boot toe. Humming a little tune, he pretended disinterest and turned to watch beyond the main street and off into the countryside. Finally, the horse couldn't take it anymore, snorted, pawed at the dust, and walked toward the clever horse trainer.

Within half an hour, Ryan was brushing the horse down, cleaning his hooves, and fitting him into his first halter.

"You just need a friend, that's all. We'll be going places and doing things before you know it."

Two hours later, after some halter work, more brushing and talking, he brought the horse into the barn and put him up in a single stall.

"It's a whole lot easier to be a good horse if you're treated right. Looks like we've both found a right nice place to hunker down, friend."

Pollack allowed himself one beer at the saloon each evening before he met the blacksmith at the café for supper. Tonight was special for Ryan Pollack.

*I love the feel and smell of a horse, and that little stud is going to be one fine animal,* he thought. *He's a smart hoss, and because of José and now Henry, I have a chance to do something good for that colt.*

On his way to the saloon, his thoughts were interrupted by loud talk. He heard breaking furniture inside the barroom. Then two gunshots rang out. Everybody on the boardwalk was looking at the establishment. A crazy-eyed hombre, holding a revolver, came crashing through the doors and onto the street. Wildly waving his pistol, the gunman threatened everyone in his way as he staggered toward some tethered horses.

"Don't nobody try to stop me," he yelled, whipping that revolver about. He struggled to untie a horse with one hand. "Stay back, I say!"

He fired a shot into the air.

The gunman had his back to the horse trainer. The fellow was still trying to untie a horse. Pollack tackled him, and the revolver fired once more. The drunken cowboy was not as big as Pollack and not as fit. Three years of busting rock makes a fellow really strong.

A left and a right with big fists knocked the head of the gun toter back and forth like a piñata at a Mexican celebration. No candy spilled, only gushes of blood from a broken nose. Three other men joined the fray, and the gunman was subdued and unarmed.

"Nice move, mister," the town lawman said, walking up. "All right, folks. The party's over. Let's get off the street now."

Henry Workman came running at the sounds of gunfire and spotted Pollack.

"Are you hurt?" yelled the blacksmith. "What happened, Ryan? You got blood all over you!"

"Not mine, Henry. Not mine," replied Pollack. "Dog gone, this was my new shirt, too. A guy shot somebody in the saloon there, and I just happened to be near enough to help catch him."

People were still milling around in the middle of the street. Several said, 'thanks' to Pollack and told the blacksmith what a brave move it took to confront the gunman.

"Ryan," said Henry, smiling proudly, "the townspeople accept you. It looks like you've found yourself a home!"

FOUR CORNERS
HOTEL
NATIONAL BANK
HARDWARE
& MINING SUPPLIES

# FOUR CORNERS

Few noticed when the tall, lanky man rode into town. After all, travel-weary men found their way to Four Corners often. Countless trails led off to all the cardinal points, taking people, bringing people, giving the town its purpose. His horse, all black but for a small star in the middle of its forehead, was tired, but residual strength remained. The animal gave the impression that it still had lots of go left in it. The rider, also tired and dusty, had that same look of inner strength about him. And the man gave a distinct impression that said, "Don't rile me, don't ask questions, stay back." He was his own man; he knew it, and others would be better off if they knew it, too.

The rider was wearing a buckskin shirt under his serape, and his hat was pushed back, showing a face that carried the lines of a man who had experienced things many other men had not. His chaps were well-worn and dirty; his boots carried silver spurs and were settled deep in stirrups. A pair of gloves was tucked in his belt, and a long Mexican reata was tied off on the saddle's left side. He wore his pistol in a cross-draw holster, and a large knife was at his waist. The man packed a lever action rifle tucked in a scabbard alongside the saddle.

Those watching thought some of his trappings indicated buckaroo, some said professional hunter, and others danger. The stranger remained silent as he dismounted in front of the hotel. He tied off the big stud, slipped the rifle out, grabbed his bedroll, and entered the old wood-framed building. At the front was the hotel desk with stairs leading up to the rooms on the second and third floors. Off to the right was a restaurant, and straight back he could see the saloon with a long oaken bar, a small stage, and gambling tables.

The stranger set his gear down, tapped the bell on the desk, and slipped a ten-dollar gold piece out of his pocket, letting it clatter onto the hardwood.

"Gonna be with us for a spell, mister?"

"Depends on how long that coin buys me a room."

"Good for a week. Take 214, straight down the hall up there, and on the right," the clerk said, handing over a large ring with a single key hanging from it. “Breakfast is served starting at five, and supper begins at four. There’s a barber shop ‘round the corner that offers hot baths.”

“Next to a cold beer, a hot bath sounds mighty good right now,” said the dusty rider.

The stranger’s smile was genuine. He nodded thanks and headed up the stairs to his room. The hotel clerk noted the deep lines in the man’s face and wondered what kinds of experiences could have made them. The clerk looked at the ledger and noted that the tall man had signed his name, Jacob Chance, Pioche, Nevada.

* * *

Chance descended the hotel stairs and went into the bar.

“I don’t get to enjoy cold beer very often,” said Chance. “Better pour another one and add a shot of corn and a cigar. I haven’t had any of those for days now.”

Jacob downed his first beer fast, then planned on enjoying the second one. As his father, Sheriff John P. Chance, always told him, “If you want information, go to the saloon keeper. They know everything that’s going on in town.”

"Bartender, you know a man named Kimble, Joshua Kimble? Heard he had a ranch in these parts."

"About twenty miles west of here, on the road to Elko," said the barkeep, "then north about ten. Don't see him much, though. Mean-tempered old man who can't keep help. If you're looking to ride for him, better think twice. Real ugly mean, that man is."

"My name's Jake Chance. I'm the deputy US Marshal up from Pioche. Nothing to get alarmed about; I'm just looking to talk to Kimble. Mean or not, I think he can help in an investigation I'm involved in. I'd appreciate it if you keep that to yourself."

"A real US Marshal, I'll be danged if I've ever met one before. Don't see no badge, though."

Chance smiled, lifted his serape, and pushed it off to the side. That shiny badge jumped out at the bartender.

"Son of a gun," said the barkeep, "a real US Marshal. You gonna stay around here and clean up this garbage pit?"

"You got a sheriff, don't ya?"

"We got a man what wears a badge, but he sure ain't no sheriff. He's one of the biggest crooks in town. Name's Aiken, Bart Aiken, and he likes to say he's just Aiken to shoot someone. He thinks that's funny."

"That's too bad," said Chance, "to hear about a crooked sheriff. I'll look into it. Anyone in town I can trust besides you, of course?"

That smile won the bartender's support.

"I might be able to introduce you to a couple of upstanding gentlemen when the evening crowd comes in."

"Thanks. Please don't mention me to the wrong people. Don't want to scare the stuffing out of the hombres I'm investigating."

Chance downed his shot of liquor, washed with the last of his beer, and headed for a hot bath and shave. He needed to scout out this place called Four Corners.

* * *

There was a feed and supply business, an arms dealer with a fine array of pistols, rifles, and scatter guns, a big hotel complex, a couple of dry goods emporiums, a blacksmith shop, a barber, and the sheriff's office and jail.

"I should stop in and say hello to the law," Chance mumbled out loud, "but it won't take long for him to know I'm here. Sheriff Aiken and Kimble, what a pair. Sticking around, they aren't very bright."

Back at the hotel, Chance went over his notes one more time. Most dealt with problems in and around Lincoln County, particularly Pioche.

*The Kimble Brothers' gang would probably still be operating in Lincoln County if they hadn't tried to rob that train,* thought Chance. *Federal offense that was, and that brought me into the picture.* Chance's musing fired up some angry memories. *That fool Peter Kimble trying to shoot me in the back while I'm watching him in a mirror. Idiot move there, and one dead Kimble to prove it. Joshua, his brother, will be a different story, I think. He's big, mean, and not totally stupid.*

Jacob Chance became a lawman because of his father and never had reason to regret the decision. He didn't want the life of a town or county sheriff and thoroughly enjoyed the freedom that came with the marshal's position.

"My territory is what I make it," he told his father, and that was the truth.

A US Marshal works at the pleasure of federal agencies such as the attorney general and, in some cases, the Military Department.

"I'll take a ride out to that Kimble ranch tomorrow, I think," said Chance, speaking to himself.

Bathed, shaved, and in clean clothes, Marshal Jake Chance went down to the saloon for a drink before supper.

* * *

"So, Marshal," whispered the bartender, "some of the stories we've heard about Sheriff Bart Aiken may be true after all? As I think back on it, it sure does make sense. Never did understand him leaving town for a week or so every once in a while. Robbing banks and trains? Not the right thing for a sheriff to do, I dare say."

Clarence Tompkins, owner of the gun shop, entered the saloon. He was introduced to Chance by the saloon keeper.

"Over the last two years," explained Marshal Chance in a low voice, "Aiken and the Kimble brothers have robbed the Lincoln County Bank twice, held up wagons carrying gold and silver from the mines and robbed the train coming into Nevada from Utah. It was carrying a large shipment of gold coins from Denver, heading to Los Angeles. That's what put me on the job. Federal offense there."

The gun shop owner and the marshal were vastly different in appearance, Tompkins being on the portly side and Chance as skinny as a hungry jackrabbit. The two men's conversation became intense.

"You've got a little problem here, Chance," said Tompkins. "With Aiken's being the sheriff in Four Corners, you can't ask for help. Most of the people in town are store clerks and such. You could get assistance from some of the buckaroos on the ranches, but they only come to town on payday. They'd be scattered all over these hills right now."

"Earlier, the saloon keeper mentioned the Kimble brothers," said Tompkins. "I only know of Josh Kimble."

"Joshua had a brother named Peter," said the marshal, "part of the gang. Fool tried to shoot me in the back, but I saw his move in a mirror and killed him. Joshua is much smarter and far meaner than old Pete was."

Chance was about to head into the restaurant when Tompkins came up with an idea.

"You can't expect to arrest Aiken and hold him in his own jail, Marshal, but I have a large room under my store that might make for a fine holding pen. I built it to keep all my guns safe when the store is closed. It's really secure and only one way in and out. If you need it, it's yours for the asking."

"Mighty obliged, Mr. Tompkins, mighty obliged. Join me for supper?"

“I’d like that, but my wife is expecting me. We live above the shop. Maybe another time.”

The two men stood up and shook hands, Tompkins heading out the big hotel doors and Chance going into the restaurant.

“Something sure smells good in here,” the lawman muttered.

Chance took a seat away from the front windows with his back to a wall. The marshal immediately saw Bart Aiken seated across the dining room with one of his deputies, his back to Chance.

This could prove interesting, thought Marshal Jacob Chance.

The marshal was nursing a large bowl of white bean and ham hock soup when one of the men he had seen in the saloon came up to his table.

“Mind a hungry dinner partner, Marshal?”

The man sat right down, not waiting for an answer. Kent Massey was one of the biggest men Chance could ever recall seeing.

“Name’s Massey, Big Dog to my friends.”

“Well, Big Dog, sit right down. Of course, you already have. You the Big Dog Blacksmith I saw a sign for?”

“That’s me, alright. Yes, sir, that’s me,” the big man answered. Then he tucked a napkin under his triple chins and held a knife in one hand and a fork in the other. "Best food in Nevada, Marshal. Best food in the West."

"I always admire a man that likes good food, Big Dog. Did you have something on your mind when you joined me?"

Before the giant could answer, the waiter brought two oversized steaks and set them in front of the blacksmith.

"Yours is coming next, Marshal," said the waiter as he turned and walked away.

"Jesse, the barkeep, said you were going to deal with Sheriff Aiken and Josh Kimble," whispered Big Dog. "I bet they're both involved in the murders and train robbin'. It's mighty good news that you are here. But I warn you, the way I see it, them two's 'bout as mean a pair's ever been drawed to. I ain't as fast as I used to be, but I'm stronger than any man in town. Can't run fur nothin' anymore, but if I gits a holt of you, you ain't goin' nowhere."

A broad smile splashed across the marshal's face, followed by a rumbling laugh.

"You and me make three of a kind, Big Dog, and three of a kind beats a pair any day of the week." The laughter of the two could be heard across the restaurant.

The men continued their sparring, enjoying every minute of it, not paying any attention to the crooked lawmen trying to stare them down.

* * *

"I hear that fellow over there is a US Marshal, Sheriff," whispered the deputy, who went by the nickname Tin Cup. "It appears he may be looking to take you and Josh back to Pioche for that train job. Want me to take him out?"

"Fool!" said Bart Aikens. "Killing a US Marshal gets you hung high and fast. Don't be stupid. We'll take him out, all right, but it has to look like an accident. Head out to Kimble's ranch at first light and let him know what's going on. And do you know where Tyson is? I could use another gun around here right now."

"He's still in Carson City prison, Bart. Got life for that bank job in Winnemucca. Killed that old lady and then shot the deputy."

"He was a good man, Tyson was," said Sheriff Aiken. "Well, I guess I'll have to make do with you and Fence. If Kimble's smart, he'll get away as fast as he can. Maybe I'll pack for a little hunting trip myself."

Marshal Chance was enjoying the lighthearted talk with Kent Massey but kept one eye on the sheriff and his deputy. He watched as the deputy stood up to leave and heard what Aiken whispered.

"Get out as early as you can in the morning and tell Kimble what's going on."

Jacob Chance lowered his voice and spoke across the table to his new acquaintance, the big blacksmith.

"How many deputies does Aiken keep around, Big Dog?"

"Usually two: that fool deputy, Tin Cup, and a man named Fence. Fence is older and used to be a gun for hire during the range wars. Some say that's where he got his name, Fence. Like Aiken, he shoots first then asks questions later. I don't think anyone has ever been arrested by these crooked lawmen; suspects die."

Chance stood up slowly, put his napkin on the table, shoved his chair back in place, and walked right up to the sheriff.

"Evening, Aiken. Finished with your supper, I hope? Keep both your hands on the table, and mind you, stand up slowly. You're under arrest for train robbery, taking coins from the US Mint, and murder. Carefully now, Aiken, so you'll live to hang."

Most of the supper crowd had already gone, and the few left moved out of the line of fire as quickly as possible. Big Dog slipped around so he was behind the crooked sheriff facing the front windows. Marshal Chance stood directly in front of Aiken.

Aiken prepared himself, then pushed hard on the table and leaped to his feet, reaching for his six-shooter. He never made it. Chance's foot slipped and he couldn't draw his pistol fast enough. The blacksmith stepped forward with the weight and strength of an ox and plastered the sheriff right behind his ear with a fist almost as large as the man's head. He was hit so hard that both feet came off the floor, and he was flung through the plate glass window and remained unconscious.

"Thought you told me you weren't fast anymore, Big Dog? Son of a gun, but that was one quick move."

"I was talkin' 'bout pullin' my guns, Marshal. Don't have that edge anymore."

That was followed by smiles from both men. Outside, they bundled Aiken up and took him to the Four Corners Gun Shop basement. There, they met the gunsmith and hog-tied the arrested sheriff.

That evening, the gun shop owner, blacksmith, and marshal walked to the saloon to put a cap on the day's events.

"I'll be heading out to Kimble's in the morning, Mr. Tompkins. Be very careful with Aiken; he's wily and dangerous."

* * *

Jake Chance was up early, had to wait a few minutes for the restaurant to open, and ordered a side of meat and potatoes. He had the cook fix him some food for the long ride, leaving before the town was awake. Chance entered Big Dog's stables to saddle up when the deputy known as Fence stepped out of the shadows.

"Hold it right there, mister," said Fence. "Who do you think you're arresting? We're going over to the gun shop, and you're going to let Bart Aiken go."

"I'm a deputy United States Marshal on official business. If you attempt to interfere with that business, you will be arrested and tried in federal court."

Chance wasn't holding anything back; he had played these cards before and knew the force of what he was saying would hold most men in check.

"We're the law here," replied Fence.

"You got no rights to interfere," said the marshal. "I'm taking the sheriff back for trial, and if you try to stop me, you'll die."

Fence was no longer in his prime, the man was a bully and killer and was paid well for his services. But now, limited to working with an equally stupid sheriff in a jerk water village on the outskirts of civilization, any edge he had was gone. Fence moved to pull his six-shooter, and his gun never cleared leather. Two shots from the marshal's forty-five ripped through the other man's chest.

"Now, that's what I call fast," Big Dog said, stepping into the stable. "I thought I heard voices. You all right, Marshal?"

Chance was bent over Fence, making sure the man was no longer a threat.

"I'm fine, Big Dog."

Now, Chance's day was changed dramatically. It's never good to start a morning by killing a man, no matter how crooked he was.

"Listen, Big Dog," said the marshal. "I need to talk to the people who run this town. I'm holding the sheriff; I just killed his deputy. If Kimble somehow hears about this, I'm sure he'll play jack rabbit on me. Can you set up some kind of meeting?"

"It's sad to say, Marshal, but we don't have any kind of town government. We just let things happen. Not smart, for sure. But there's the hotel owner, bartender, me, the gunsmith, and maybe old Doc Harkin. What did you have in mind?"

"A town like this needs leadership, Big Dog. Without people taking part in running their community, you end up with people like Aiken running you. You folks are going to have to fill that void soon; otherwise, some other Aiken will move in."

Chance began saddling the black stud while he was talking, and as he led the horse out of the barn and stepped into the saddle, he nodded to Big Dog.

"I don't like to tell people what to do or how to do it, but best to keep Aiken locked up, fed, and watered. I'll be back either late tonight or early tomorrow morning. Put that meeting together if you can. I really do want to talk to those people who can make things happen. You've got a nice little town here and an opportunity to make it better."

With that, the US Marshal nudged the stud lightly and urged him to a steady trot, one that the big black could keep up all day.

* * *

Marshal Jacob Chance liked to talk to himself as he rode and put things together. This morning, he had lots of time to do that.

"I sounded an awful lot like my father back there," he said to the black, that was moving fast. "With a little direction, that village could be a nice place to live. A mayor, a town council, an honest sheriff, a school and a church, and Four Corners would be a good home."

The Ruby Mountains loomed to the marshal's left as he turned north to meet the outlaw Joshua Kimble.

*Interesting, now that I think about it,* he mused. *That Fence was in town this morning. Did he ride all the way out here last night and then ride all the way back? I don't think so. Maybe Kimble doesn't know I'm coming.*

The marshal slowed the big stud down to a walk.

"Ease it off, big boy. We both want to be in pretty good shape when we find Kimble."

Large white and gray clouds roiling with thunder and rain were moving towards him as the day's heat continued to build. The Nevada desert can be explosively oppressive and deadly but always magnificent. Finding a catch basin filled with water wasn't unusual. Many ranchers dug out natural wells for their stock. Finding one has saved many a buckaroo and animal.

"See all that green over there, hoss? Let's go get a nip or two of water?"

The marshal turned his horse off the trail towards bright green vegetation. He found a pond and spring on a little hillside. He dismounted and lead his horse to water and let him drink. A couple of miles down the trail, he saw the Kimble ranch.

"How's that for good luck," he muttered to his horse.

He ground-hitched the stud in a patch of grass and hunkered down with a long spyglass he always carried.

"I'll be darned, somebody's home," he said quietly. He could see two saddled horses tied up at the front of the main house. "He isn't planning to run off. If he was, he'd have a pack on one of those mounts."

* * *

"Listen, I'm trying to tell you what I saw last night," said the sheriff's deputy. "The guy called himself a US Marshal. He had dinner with Big Dog, and they arrested Aiken and are holding him. Fence was supposed to come out here, but I saw him later, and he told me to do it. This marshal is going to take you in, Mr. Kimble. I rode all night to warn you."

"Well, Tin Cup, you did good. Go on, get yourself a whiskey. Ain't no US Marshal gonna take me down. What did he look like, tall and thin, wearing a serape?"

"Yeah, that's him, Mr. Kimble," he said, pouring a healthy cup of the amber liquid.

The Tin Cup moniker came from the deputy's habit of carrying a cup on his belt and mooching drinks off anyone nearby. His real name was Thomas Gomez, and most men he met never knew that. Normally, Tin Cup hadn't held a job for more than an hour—that is until he became Sheriff Aiken's deputy.

"Kimble, I got to tell you, that lawman looked real mean."

"He's the marshal that shot my brother," said Kimble. "I hope he does come out here and tries to take me. Putting a few slugs in his ugly carcass would be a real pleasure. He killed Pete in cold blood."

Tin Cup was about to pour a second shot but was holding back some.

"Go ahead, Tin Cup, have another, and then get out of here. I don't want no witnesses when I kill that lawman. Get on your horse and go."

"Thank you, Mr. Kimble." The deputy swallowed his drink, ran out the door, got on his horse, and turned back to Four Corners.

Through his spyglass, the lawman watched Tin Cup leave.

* * *

Marshal Chance turned his black off the road into the sage. He used all the cover he could find to stay out of sight as he moved towards the ranch.

"I guess that means Kimble knows I'm coming," Chance whispered to his horse. "That's the deputy who was with Sheriff Aiken in the restaurant."

The marshal stepped off the stud and tied him to a scrub of sage. Rifle in hand, he moved slowly toward the ranch house. The lawman was hunkered down about a hundred yards away when Kimble came out the front door with a rifle. Chance let him come down off the porch and spoke before the man could get on his horse.

"Hold it right there, Kimble. Drop that rifle!"

Chance was well-hidden, and Kimble couldn't find him. Then, the wanted man saw movement in the brush. The outlaw pulled the rifle up to his shoulder and aimed it at the lawman. The marshal was quicker. His shot rang out, echoing through the hot desert air. Kimble fell to the ground, firing his rifle into the dirt. The outlaw bled out before Chance could get to him.

"You didn't have to get shot, Kimble. All you had to do was drop the rifle."

Taking his time, the marshal tied the body across the saddle of the outlaw's horse. Mounting his own, Chance started the long journey back to Four Corners. He had reached the Elko road when he saw a group of riders coming toward him.

"This could be bad, hoss," he said, moving the horses off the trail and into deep sage.

The lawman pulled his rifle, made sure there was a bullet in the chamber, and waited.

*That skinny little deputy could not have gotten back to town that fast*, thought Chance. *I hope those town people haven't done something foolish like letting Aiken out. Whatever it is, I'm ready.*

He could see at least five riders in the bunch, and then he saw Big Dog in the lead. He moved the horses back onto the main road and waited. Tin Cup was in the group, his arms tied behind his back.

* * *

It was a gathering of six riders and one dead man led by Big Dog and Marshal Jake Chance, who rode into Four Corners a few hours later. Storekeepers, bartenders, barbers, and even old Doc were on the streets welcoming them back. The gunsmith Tompkins was standing in the middle of the street, wearing a big shiny star and revealing himself as sheriff.

"After you left this morning, Marshal," said Big Dog Massey, "I woke everybody up early and told them what you said. Amazing how quickly it went, and then four of us formed a posse to come help you."

Big Dog sat astride a Belgian draft horse while talking to the marshal. It was evident even that huge horse was suffering under the enormous weight of the blacksmith.

"Clarence is our new sheriff," said Big Dog. "And now he has his first two men behind bars, and they appointed me mayor. Can you imagine that?"

Chance stayed another couple of days. He helped get all the legal matters taken care of, then bundled up his prisoner and prepared to head back to Pioche. The entire town turned out for the marshal's departure.

"Never let your guard down," said Chance, "and I figure you'll have a nice, quiet, friendly community."

Big Dog put that large beefy hand out. It swallowed Chance's. The blacksmith squeezed tight and the lawman winced. The new mayor let go and smiled.

"We made some bad mistakes," said Big Dog, "but, Marshal, we're going in the right direction now. I've asked three of the cowhands from the Lazy Seven to meet you and ride guard back to Pioche."

"Mighty obliged," replied Marshal Chance.

"You come back to Four Corners any time you want," said Tompkins, the new lawman.

"Yes, any time," agreed Big Dog.

# NOT THIS TIME

The dust from seven hundred steers boiled into the hot desert air as Sam Poster watched from a rise just west of the herd.

"Them two jaspers still followin'?" the rancher Sam Poster asked his trail foreman, Doc Jensen.

"Can't see 'em right now for the dust, but they was with us when we moved out this mornin'," drawled Doc, rolling a cigarette while taking a short break. "They be waitin' for somethin', but I don't understand what two men could do."

"Spread the word for the hands to keep a sharp eye out, Doc. Two men ain't gonna steal this herd, but they be up to somethin' for sure," replied the ranch owner.

Sam moved his horse into a gentle lope down off the rise to join the herd. Doc ground out his butt on his chaps and trotted off, following the boss.

*What are those fellows doin'?* thought Doc. *Of course they could be waitin' for others down the line. Ain't gonna worry about it none until the shootin' starts.*

Sam Poster moved his steers every year from his ranch. They followed the long wide open plain more than a hundred miles to the railhead. There his cattle were loaded on stock cars and headed east for the butcher's block. According to folks around the area, Poster's drive was always the first one of the year. His cattle usually the fattest and best offering at the stockyards.

Doc Jensen ordered the herd bunched up in some tall grass for the evening, set his night hawks, and joined Poster at the chow wagon.

"Even if them fools are gonna try to rustle this herd, what the heck good would it do them?" Doc asked his boss. "Only place to sell them would be the stockyards at the railhead. Everyone knows they'd be your cattle. Don't make no sense, Mr. Poster. No sense a'tall."

Doc had a tin cup of coffee balanced on a knee, rolled a cigarette and lit it, and rested his back on a wagon wheel.

"Did they ride near enough to see the whole herd?" Poster asked his foreman.

"Might have. I tried to get close to those riders," replied the foreman, "but they be clever jaspers, stayin' just far enough back."

Then the rancher took a piece of pie from the cook, tasted it and said, "Mighty fine! You bribin' me for somethin', Cookie?"

* * *

The two mysterious riders shadowed the herd all the way to the stockyards. After the count, Poster got paid. He called his buckaroos together at their camp just outside the little rail stop.

"That was a good drive, boys. Only lost a couple of calves and didn't have any trouble. Doc Jensen has your pay and I want you back at the ranch as soon as possible. Enjoy yourselves, don't get throwed in jail."

That brought lots of chuckles and snickers, finger pointing, and elbowing.

"Have fun boys!" was the ranch boss's final words.

Doc handed out the envelopes and then joined the riders on their way to town. The cow hands headed for whiskey, hot baths, and painted ladies. Rancher Sam Poster spent a quiet evening in camp, doing some paper work and watching the stars move about.

“Made some good money on this drive,” he said quietly, putting the gold coins, paper bills, and ledger into a tin box and locking it.

“When we headin’ back, boss?” Cookie asked, sticking his head in Poster’s tent, offering some more of his honey biscuits.

“We’ll go into town in the morning and get the supplies we need. We’ll find Doc and as many boys that want to ride back with us. We should be well out of town by sunset. Hopefully by evening, we’ll make camp at the river. Glad it’ll only take half the time to reach the ranch.”

Camp was packed by seven the next morning with rowdy cowboys that hadn’t slept the night.

Sam Poster and Cookie took the wagon into the little village. They rode up to the supply store and Cookie did the ordering.

“I’ll find Doc and the rest of the hands that want to go with us and meet you right here, Cookie. It’s easier to get the supplies now, so make sure you purchase what you need.”

Then the ranch boss trotted down the street toward the saloon and a nearby café.

“Doc will be in one or the other,” Poster chuckled out loud.

Seeing all his cattle in the pens stretched out along the south side of the town was a great satisfaction. The rail lines on the other side of the pens gleamed under the morning sun. Poster found his foreman and three buckaroos in the café. The hungry cowhands were carving up steaks and potatoes.

"Right on time, boss," Doc said as Poster sat down.

"Just coffee for me," the rancher told the waitress. "You boys a bit hungry, are you?" He laughed sizing up the platters. "Cookie won't want to hear about this."

"Who's gonna tell him?" laughed one of the cowhands.

"Not me," said another.

"Any pie?" asked Poster as the young lady set his coffee down.

She returned with a large piece of blackberry pie and refilled everyone's cup.

"Nice to see cowboys eat," she said. "You boys work hard and eat good. I like that."

She smiled as she walked back to the kitchen.

"Soon's the wagon's loaded, Doc, we'll be heading back," said Poster. "You boys coming along?"

Doc answered for them.

"Yeah, these jaspers and a couple more, gettin' a hot bath before we head out. You get your bath yet, boss?"

"No. We'll be at the river tonight. Cold water is good enough for these old bones," he said.

The three buckaroos pretended to shiver.

* * *

About two hours later, Cookie on the chuck wagon, the ranch owner, the foreman, and three cowhands rode out of town. The old wagon groaned with its heavy load.

"Bout bought the place out, didn't you, Cookie?" Poster joked.

They made it back to their camp and roused the sleeping and hungover cowhands, packed up, and headed back. Late in the day, they made it to the river. Cookie was busy fixing supper, Poster briefly bathed in the cold water, and the men worked on their gear.

"Be ready to rise early, boys," said the ranch owner. "I want to get home. These drives are lasting far too long."

The horses, back from the water, were grazing on good grass in a rope corral. One rider guarded them, and everybody else laid out their bedrolls. Several hours later Doc was awakened by faint noises. He saw men moving past the horses and the guard. Doc grabbed his rifle, got up, and shook Sam Poster awake and pointed.

"You hombres freeze," shouted the rancher.

One of the intruders fired a pistol at the voice coming from the dark. Both Doc and Poster took careful aim with their rifles and fired.

Within seconds, the entire camp was awake. The horses broke free from the guard and the rope enclosure and stampeded into the dark. Poster's rifle was smoking from his first shot. Sandy Morales, a tough cowhand, cussed both in Spanish and English and dropped two men as they came at him with rifles. Doc picked up his reata and raced toward the last horse that was tangled in rope. With his reata around the animal's neck, he untangled kicking hooves, got the horse upright and mounted bareback. Using heels and knees, the foreman galloped across the open prairie, after the horse herd. A long time later, the foreman returned with most of the spent mounts.

Rounding up the the frightened mustangs was the hardest part of the fray. After the altercation,

Cookie got a big fire going. Lamps were lit, and buckaroos walked around determining which outlaws were alive or dead. The cowhands gathered at the fire, guns in hand.

"Bring the live ones over here and the dead ones over there," ordered Poster and pointed to the fire.

"Let's find out who these fine, upstanding citizens might be."

Two men with bullet wounds sat in front of the fire. One was bleeding out, the other nursing a wound to his right thigh. Five dead bodies were stretched out in the sand on the other side of the fire. Their personal belongings were set on the ground in front of them.

"Well, Doc," said Sam Poster, "looks like we know why those two were following. Why rustle if you can just wait and steal the money?"

Knives, pistols, and a couple of rifles were in the pile. They checked wallets for identification and found nothing.

"You boys aren't going to last long," said Poster. "Want to tell me who you are?"

There was no response.

"No?" exclaimed Poster.

The rancher was going to prod the fellow with the leg wound when the other outlaw toppled over. He almost fell into the fire.

"Check him, Doc," ordered Poster.

"He's dead, boss," said Doc.

"Might as well hang that other one," said the rancher. "He don't get to die from just a leg wound."

Poster poked the outlaw with a rifle. "Sure you don't have anything to say?"

Again, no response. The wounded outlaw was holding his leg and trying to stop the bleeding.

"Sandy Morales got a nick in his side from a bullet," exclaimed Cookie, "but, I got him patched up. We're darn lucky no one else got hurt."

"If it wasn't for you, Doc," said Morales in a thick Spanish accent, "we would have lost all them horses. We're gonna have to put one down. Busted up a leg pretty bad."

"All right, let's get the dead ones buried," ordered the rancher. "Use that pine over there, and hang this fool."

"You can't do that!" exclaimed the wounded outlaw.

"You tried to rob us, then shoot us—now take your medicine," replied Sam Poster.

After the hanging, the boss spoke to his men.

"Let's head back to the ranch, boys. Sure wish we had a name from at least one of these hombres. When we get back, we'll tell the Rangers about this. Too bad we got outlaws all over these plains. At least this bunch is not getting anything—not this time—not ever."

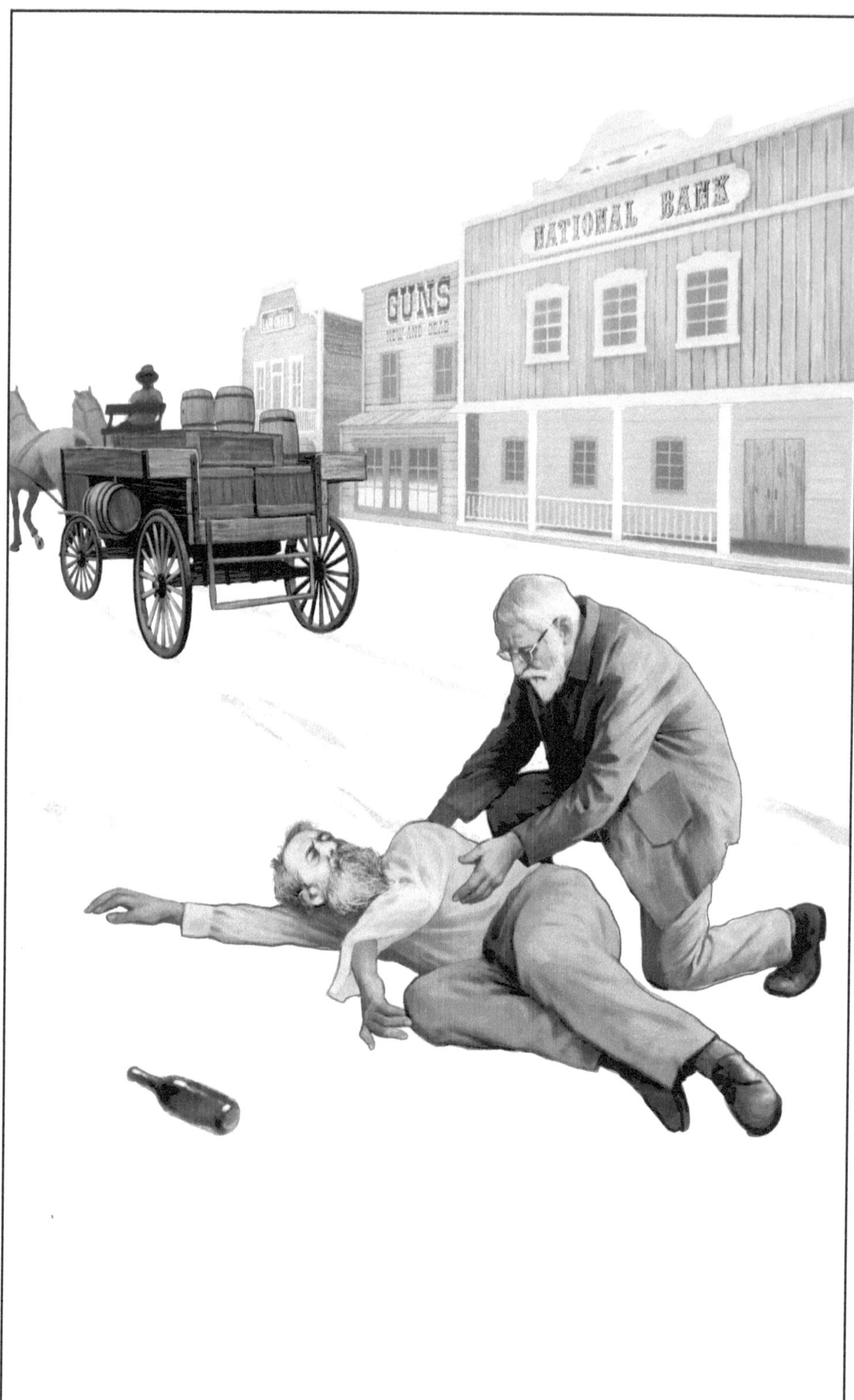
NATIONAL BANK
GUNS

# OLD SAM AND THE WAGON

Old Sam Gephardt limped his way across the muddy main street. It was a cold, windy, miserable early spring morning. He headed for his first stop along saloon alley in Rim Rock for a 'wake-me-up' draught of rotgut whiskey. He knew he should stop at Ramon's Bakery and beg for a day-old biscuit, but the thought of blazing hot whiskey pouring down a dry throat was far more overpowering.

Old Sam wasn't that old; those who had been in Rim Rock for a spell knew that. It was the whiskey and a hard life that made the geezer look ancient. One arm was forever bent, the elbow knotted up after being broken twice and never properly set. His left leg straight as an arrow, the knee fused after being crushed by a crazed bull during a roundup years ago. And his right leg was gimpy from the same accident.

Old Sam entered the saloon, his body further paining him for the need of alcohol. Having no money, he talked to the patrons about being a buckaroo on the Nevada ranches. Then he spoke about gun-slingin' in Dead Horse, Wyoming Territory. A few drinks under his belt, and he bragged about riding with Pancho Villa. The more Sam talked, the more his listeners would buy, and by noon, the broken-down westerner was plastered.

To a certain extent, those who ran the saloons loved the old man because he was good for business. That is until he got that last one, which put him over the top; then Old Sam got belligerent, feisty, and obnoxious. The kind of drunk that can clear a saloon in seconds, and then they tossed him out. He'd been known to sleep in the mud for an hour, then start in on the next saloon in line. By the end of the day, he was not welcome in any of them. Like everything in his life, Old Sam Gephardt gave it his all. And now, he was the hardest-drinking man anyone had ever seen.

But, on this morning, things were different. Sam made it to about the middle of the muddy street when a wagon, piled high with produce and mechanical devices of all kinds, pulled by four big draft horses, came barreling down the narrow street.

Did the driver not see Old Sam? Did the driver not care? Were those coursers out of control? Old Sam was struck dead on. He was smacked down onto his back. He splashed into the mud and was run over by the large wagon wheels. Those who were first on the scene were amazed that the old man was still alive. For sure, they thought they would have to carry his skinny carcass off for burial on Potter's Hill.

The doctor found broken bones, ripped muscles, torn cartilage, and cuts and bruises on every part of Old Sam. Contusions went deep inside the wrinkled and pocked skin of the old man. The pain must have been tremendous. Those weeks in the hospital were far harder on the medical staff than on Sam. It was the alcohol withdrawals and not the accident he suffered the most from. This included him seeing hundreds of snakes infesting his room and bed, wild animals attacking nightly, and visions of spiders and scorpions. Worst was his loud, angry, and incessant demands for "just one stinkin' drink"!

Toward the end of the second week, he found himself telling very lucid stories to some of those trying their best to tend to him. They learned that he had been a lawman in the Dakota Territories, had helped open some of the most famous cattle trails out of Texas, and really did fight with Pancho Villa. His attitude changed daily, from an angry old drunk to what one might call a sociable, somewhat educated, almost gentleman-like human. He was eating well, getting just enough exercise to not interfere with his healing, and found that he had some friends in the world after all.

Doc Simpson was fully aware that as soon as Old Sam left the medical building, he would walk two muddy blocks to Saloon Alley and become a drunken reprobate once again. Doc believed that all men were good despite forty years of medical practice, where he met some of the worst and most challenging cases the West had to offer. After weeks of conversations with a sober and lucid Sam, the doctor wanted to do something right for the old coot.

One day, Doc changed his conversation to a different subject. He told Sam that if he felt strong enough, he had a job waiting for him at the old Triple Y out in Tuscarora, Nevada. They needed a line cook, and Doc knew Sam had been one for years. You'd be back in the saddle, old man, or at least in a line camp among cowboys, Doc told him. Surprisingly, Sam responded the right way.

"Come to think of it, I'd like to be back on the open range," said Sam, smiling. "You know, Doc, I am a good cook."

"Sam," said the doctor, "that's great."

* * *

"You're a cheater, Doc," said Old Sam the next morning. "I been thinkin' on it, and I know the Triple Y is owned by the Mormons. I won't be able to even put a shot of whiskey in the chili!"

Doc Simpson smiled for weeks after sending Old Sam off to his new life.

# SANDY'S TALL TALE

Little Sandy MacTavish stands only about four feet, seven inches, and has probably never weighed more than seventy pounds in his entire life, which at this moment measures nigh onto seventy-three years.

"Actually, boys, me fightin' weight is sixty-two and one-half pounds. Or there–a—boot."

Sandy MacTavish is a bit of a rounder from the old school, a real dust-buster, if you must know.

"In me younger days, lads, there wasn't a wee lass that was safe. And the young ladies so darlin' and warm. Ah! Growin' old fer a man like me... well, lads, it's bound to happen to you too, but it's such a pity! Such a pity!"

His eyes wandered skyward when he said it. As if praying for a younger self or a few more lasses. Sandy MacTavish rode the horses in Ireland, Scotland, and Great Britain, had pictures to prove it, and even raced in the Kentucky Derby. Many a glorious night we've spent over a drink or two looking at the faded fifty-year-old pictures. We all heard the many stories and shared in his triumphs.

He was primed for a story tonight, and nothing would slow him down—except maybe a short pause here and there 'to wet the chords, you know,' he regaled us.

"I wis down ta the governor's office yestidy, and the man asked me to lunch with him. I up and tells this fine man that it's very close to the end of the month, ya know, and me resources may not be up to lunching with the gentry. The governor, lads, I'm not making this up, he delves into one of his pants's pockets and comes up with one hundred dollars. That fine gentleman passes me that C note and says, 'Let's have some fun with that young upstart senator who's joining us, and you demand to pay for lunch.' That's what he said, on me sainted mother's grave, that's what he said.

"Well, lads, here I am, Sandy MacTavish, late of Edinburgh, ridin' in the back seat of the governor's limo, the guv on one side of me, and that Senator Lauck on t'other. And lads, I'm saying, 'Governor, it's been too long since I've had the honor. I'm takin' us to lunch today.' Mr. Smith, he's the driver you know, says, 'Let's eat at the Rainbow Grill.'

"I noticed right away the senator kind of tensed up, but me friend, the governor, smiled and said something about it bein' a kind gesture, and lunch at the Rainbow would be excellent.

"I had a bowl of delicious barley soup and the sweetest piece of cod ever. We all drank a glass or two of some excellent white wine, and it was a merry lunch, indeed. In fact, the young lass who was serving us this fine repast even commented on what good taste we had. She was something to see, boys. Something to see.

"The senator, I keep remembering, was trying to make a point with the governor, and then the governor would lightly kick me in the shin. I picked up on that right away and started telling stories—you know, about the old days and the horses and the ladies. You lads know how I like to talk about the horses, how a man could read bloodlines and trainers and actually make a pleasant living by betting a quid or two from time to time.

"That C note just covered lunch and a wee bit for the lovely lass who served us. She gave a special kind of thank you smile to me. So, when I was leaving the governor's office, he handed me a 20. 'What's this?' I demanded, and the governor said I saved him from a terrible problem. The senator, it seems, wanted the governor's approval to bring forth a bill to end off–track betting in this state.

"Boys, lunch with a world-renowned jockey, and all me tall tales, changed his mind! I've got a hot twenty here in me hands, lads, and I think we'll all have a drink right now on Senator Lauck."

# SIGN TALKER

They called him Dusty more because of his appearance than anything else. He was always covered with a layer of trail dust that would defy imagination. He wasn't much at socializing, didn't belly up to the bar with the rest of the trail-weary bunch in the saloon, and rarely spoke to anyone. Rather, he grunted out something or babbled incoherently. If he had a real name, no one knew it, and no one cared.

One exception was Marlene Jacobson, the nice little old lady who was married to the Mexican who ran the café.

"José, I want you to bring that Dusty back in here. He left about ten minutes ago. I may have learned something watching him try to tell me the mush was too hot."

Dusty never said actual words, just a jumble of noises, and at the café, he simply pointed at the menu. When people didn't understand the sounds that came out of his mouth, he got upset, moving his hands and his gibberish getting louder. It seemed no one made sense of the noises he made.

José nodded his head and walked away. He had had more than one run-in with the man but began to do what he was ordered. Then he stopped and spoke to his wife.

"You can't talk to that man, Marlene. No one understands a word he says. What in the heck did you see?"

"You just bring him back, and I'll show you."

José scuttled out the door and down the long street. He figured Dusty would be somewhere near the livery or blacksmith shop. He found him lighting a cigar at the smithy's forge.

"Marlene wants to see you, Dusty. Better get back down to the café. You know how impatient she can be." He spun on his heel and walked across the street to the saloon for a pick-me-up. "I'm not gonna listen to his nonsense this morning," he muttered, stepping through the heavy front doors.

Dusty shuffled his way down to the café, wondering what he had done this time. Nobody ever wanted to talk to him unless he had done something wrong.

"Sit down, Dusty," said Marlene. "Want a cup of joe?"

He nodded yes, sat down, took off his floppy old sombrero, and snuffed out the cigar. Marlene frowned on people smoking in the café or wearing their hats at the table. She brought two cups of steaming coffee and joined the old man.

"How old are you, Dusty, about fifty?" asked the woman.

She looked into his very bright eyes as he nodded yes to her question. Then she did something that surprised the man so much he almost jumped out of his chair. She asked the same question in Indian sign language, something she had learned as a child while living near Fort Bridger. Most of her friends had been from the Crow and Blackfeet tribes in the area.

The old man collected himself and settled into his chair, again answering her in the affirmative, using sign language. They sat across from each other, both with grand smiles on their faces, fingers and hands flying. Both chuckled. They became more animated and then a bit more controlled in their sign talk. Their eyes danced with joy at being able to communicate.

Two or three late customers had come in. Marlene took care of them and returned to the table with Dusty as quickly as possible. It became quite a show. After a while, people gathered around the table to watch these two making their hand gestures, even laughing from time to time. One of the patrons left the café and hurried to a saloon down the street.

Old Jack Crockett hurried up to José at the bar.

"You aren't going to believe what's going on down to the café. I've never seen the like. Marlene and Dusty flingin' their hands around, laughin'. It's somethin' to see."

José downed his morning bracer and hurried back to his restaurant.

He was just in time to see Dusty make some kind of weird gesture, and Marlene broke out in a fit of laughter. She looked up at her husband with a flashing smile.

"What the heck is going on?" José asked.

"Sit down, José, and listen to this story. No, grab some coffee for all of us first, then sit down."

Coffee was poured, and everyone stood silent and listened. By now, there was quite an interested crowd of Westerners. Marlene began to tell what she had learned.

"Dusty was kidnapped by the Lakota when he was a boy of about ten and raised as a slave. He learned sign language and lived as an Indian well into his early twenties when he escaped and made his way to a town," Marlene said. She stopped long enough to take a healthy swig of hot coffee and continued. "See that horrible scar on his face? An arrow went through his cheek, ripped his tongue out, and he almost died. That's why he can't talk and why he only eats really soft food."

"Wife, you always amaze me," exclaimed José.

"He can read a few words but doesn't know how to write. For all these years, he's only been able to make sounds. Not many people know how to sign as the Indians do. It's lucky that I can. José, this man has so many wonderful stories to tell. He has a fine sense of humor, and I'm going to teach him how to read and write."

The story flew up and down Main Street. Within two hours, all forty-seven people in Little Bend heard some version of it. Dusty had a new and welcoming reputation. Marlene was an excellent teacher and put Dusty to work in the café. He washed dishes, cut firewood, swamped out evenings, and learned how to read and write at night.

* * *

"I can't tell you just how intelligent this man is, José. It's been six months, and he can read and write very well. He learns everything I teach him quickly."

With money coming in regularly, finding himself living under a roof and not out in the open, Dusty cleaned himself up. A hot bath once a week, a shave, and a haircut from time to time, and Dusty was a changed man. For the first time, he wore a smile. He carried a little notebook and pencil with him and was able to communicate with those who could read and write.

Dusty made friends with one gentleman in particular. David P. Christopher put out a newspaper for the communities up and down the river. Flat Creek was some ten miles upriver from Little Bend, and Ox-Bow was about fifteen miles down. Because of the river, Christopher could deliver his newspaper by canoe each week.

Dusty had the morning chores done around the café when Christopher came in.

"Marlene, will you and Dusty join me for a cup of coffee? I have an interesting proposition."

David P. Christopher was a man full of himself. This morning, his little pencil mustache was almost dancing with nervous excitement. The man always had his hair slicked back. He took immense pride in the frock suit he always wore. He pulled a crumpled letter from his coat pocket, smoothed it, and handed it to Marlene. She sat down to read.

"Dusty will be famous!" the newspaperman exclaimed giving both the woman and Dusty a big smile.

Marlene scanned the document. She looked at David P. Christopher as if to ask if this was for real. Then handed the missive to Dusty. He read it and looked up.

"My friend in New York," explained Christopher, "runs a book publishing company. As you can see from that letter, when I told him about Dusty, that's what he wrote back. He wants Dusty to write in his own words about his life and the exciting stories he has told some of us. We agreed if I publish them in a column in the paper every week, Mr. Burbank in New York will turn those stories into a book. If Dusty is willing, I'll pay him the going rate for that column, and Mr. Burbank will offer him a book contract that could be worth a lot of money."

For several moments, it remained very quiet at the table. Dusty reread the letter and then again once more. He looked at Marlene. Then he signed to her.

"I'm so glad you're a sign-talker. Tell Mr. Christopher I accept." He smiled and added, "I already have lots of stories written. But he doesn't need to know that."

The two chuckled. Dusty wrote on a piece of paper and handed it across the table to the newspaperman.

*"Thank you!"*

# A FINE DRIVE

The rising sun burned the late-season frost off the sagebrush. Sam Tyson looked up into the deep blue of a Nevada spring morning and smiled. He let the last drop of coffee slowly slip down his throat. Raising his right hand, he brushed early morning dew from both sides of his thick, drooping mustache.

"Gonna be a fine day to move these cows up into the high hills. A fine day, indeed."

The lazy ST sprawled along the Humboldt River in north central Nevada, covering open range for a couple of thousand acres, and shared space with deer, antelope, big horn sheep, quail, sage hen, and rabbits. There were enough coyotes to keep a range rider busy, and in the timber, one might very well run into a mountain lion or two. Ground squirrels and badgers put enough holes in the ground to ruin more than one good horse each season, and rattlesnakes seem to know just when to mess with your mind.

"Beautiful," old Sam muttered, stepping into the saddle and settling down onto the back of a fine stud. At a brisk trot, he rode out to where his crew had a herd of about a thousand head of cows and steers. They were ready to hit the trail for the five days it would take to get them into high summer pasture. With no pressure on the mecate, the bosal lightly in place, Sam swung the stud into line with his foreman and range boss, Tweed Johnson.

"What do you smell, Tweed?" he asked as the two rode together toward the head of the herd. "Got rain in those nostrils of yours?"

"We'll be in the last of the white stuff in two days, boss. It was a good winter with heavy snow up there. Means a wet spring and summer. Yup, I do smell rain, but not 'til it gets a bit warmer. Need that heat to make those thunderstorms." He smiled, knowing that Tyson already knew everything he had just said. "We'll hit mud and some running creeks up higher. I already spread the word to keep the herd in tight. Get 'em runnin' in that mud, and we get injured animals."

The foreman raised his right arm high and gave the signal to start the herd moving.

"Been a cold winter, Tweed," said Sam Tyson. "This drive will be good for my old bones. Sunshine, high mountain air, so sweet and warm, and nothing like a good open cooking fire. This will straighten me right out."

Sam Tyson came to this country back in the early 1850s when he was in his twenties and built the ST from an open desert to a thriving cattle ranch. Nearing eighty, the old man was wondering if this would be his last spring drive.

"All these years, Tweed, and I still tingle with anticipation every spring. Only missed one drive, back when that fool horse fell on me and broke both my legs, and what a miserable summer that was."

"I bet," replied Tweed.

Sam laughed, remembering how frustrated he was, just sitting on the porch all day with both legs in casts from his crotch to his heels.

"All these years, and what I remember and regret most, is the drive I didn't do."

There were smiles on the faces of both men.

The next several hours were filled with getting the herd lined up, keeping it together, and teaching the young steers to stay close to mama. They followed the well-worn trail that would lead them ten miles a day into the high mountains, the peaks still snow-capped in the last of the winter's cloak.

Many of the buckaroos changed horses at mid-day break, but not old Sam. A biscuit of hard tack and some cold meat from a coat pocket, washed down with canteen water, and the old rancher and his herd continued its plodding march.

First night along the trail is always a little anxious. The herd wants to go back home or anyplace other than where they were—the young calves curious and rambunctious. The routine of setting up camp is slow.

"What do you think, Tweed?" said the old rancher. "Good day, I'd say."

Sam Tyson squatted down near a small fire in front of his tent. He had a tin plate full of hot stew in one hand and a tin cup filled with coffee in the other. He set the coffee down, pulled a spoon from his shirt pocket, and took a full measure of stew.

"Just right," said Sam. "Hey, Cookie!" he yelled across the open area. "Darn good chuck!"

He got a friendly wave back.

"Tweed, remember the year the night hawks quit us in the middle of the night?" asked the ranch boss. "Just rode off and took about fifty nice calves with them. Spent two years rounding those boys up. No real law around back then, so...well...we strung 'em up, pinned signs on their bodies that simply said, 'rustler,' and left 'em for the vultures and ravens."

The foreman nodded.

"Had to do things that way, Tweed. Area's a bit more civilized today, I guess, but still...we are on our own. Man's got to take care of his business."

Tyson's foreman had been on the ranch for a lot of years and was as close to the old man as a son might be. The foreman nodded again in full agreement as the boss talked and reminisced.

"It wasn't just a few years ago when we had to drive our cattle to what they called a market," continued Sam. "Elko was the destination, but that didn't make much sense 'cause the population was in Reno and Virginia City."

"Do ya reckon that might be why they built the railroad, Sam?" asked Tweed.

"Sure. When we bring these steers and cows back down come fall, them cattle will be fat and ready for the feed yard, and that railroad will haul 'em off. But, I sure do miss those old trail rides."

The two men talked into the night and finally went to their bedrolls, snoring up a storm. Sunrise came early for old Sam Tyson.

"I can feel every mile of the trail this morning," grumbled the old rancher, pouring a tin cup full of boiling coffee. "Just give me a biscuit and some side meat this morning, Cookie. I'm still full of that stew from last night."

"Let me put some bacon grease gravy over those biscuits, boss," said Cookie. "Long ride today, you need your strength."

Cookie chuckled, knowing Sam Tyson never turned down biscuits and gravy on the trail or at the main ranch.

Mornings around a trail drive camp were hectic and filled with action: horses raising a ruckus, buckaroos talking loud and long, cattle bawling and stomping, and orders being given in every direction. Tyson sat on a stool alongside the chuck wagon, sopping up hot gravy, smiling broadly as he watched all the activity. His eye drifted up into the clear sky and picked out a couple of ravens doing their own brand of ballet, and then he watched a young buckaroo try to throw a saddle on a young gelding not quite ready to be saddled. His laughter was infectious as Cookie joined in the vista.

"Mornings are something special, eh Cookie?" said Sam. "Look at all that action out there. I think people would pay just to watch this if it happened in a city somewhere. Good gravy, by the way." Sam chuckled, wiping the last little bit from his plate. "Remember a few years ago when some fool buckaroo shot off his pistol, and the whole herd came through camp just as you were puttin' grub on the plates? What a show that was! Wiped out the wagon, tore up everybody's teepees, horses running amok. What a show!"

And yet again, the old man was filled with humor.

"I don't think I used the word show, boss. No, sir, that wasn't one of the words I used that morning."

Both men were laughing hard as Tweed walked up to fill his coffee cup.

"You two are sure having fun. No injuries to cows or men, boss. We'll be ready to move out shortly. Want me to saddle up for you?"

"No. You take care of the cattle and the men, Cookie will take care of the wagon, and I'll saddle my own horse," said the old man, just a bit gruff, then smiled, loosening up some. "It kind of goes with the territory, Tweed."

The old ranch boss walked over to watch the camp boys tear down the canvas tents, roll up the bedrolls, and put everything in the wagon.

"Good work, boys," said Sam. "Make sure Cookie gets everything he wants and get plenty of wood along the ride. As we get higher, the nights will be a lot colder." The hustle was slowing down around the camp as Sam saddled the stud and mounted for another long day.

"I can smell the mountains," said Sam, "smell the air getting thinner, feel the changes. Gosh, I love a trail drive." His muttering to himself had been a way of life for a long time. "There's just one thing missing from all this. I should have married that little Shoshone girl years ago. Mighta had sons and daughters riding with us every year."

Those thoughts stayed with him most of the day. After supper that night, with a fire blazing in front of his tent, he brought the subject up with Tweed.

"Shoulda married that pretty little Running Antelope," he said. "Well, that's a whole 'nother story, eh? I'm thinkin' it's about time to take up whittlin' or something."

"You'd get excited and cut a finger off," Tweed chuckled, settling down by the fire. "Herd's moving along fine, weather's good, and Cookie's fixin' some mighty tasty grub. This sure ain't the time to tuck 'er in."

"'Member a few years ago?" said Sam. "Cookie got all upset and angry at us cuz we didn't tell him at every opportunity how good his food was? Darn near poisoned the whole crew, Tweed." The old man rocked back and forth, laughing. "Good chuck, Cookie. Good chuck," he hollered over toward the wagon.

Sam and Tweed heard some grumbling coming from that direction and laughed some more among themselves.

"Oh, how I do love these trail drives. We've only been out two days, and I'm feeling this one," Tyson muttered, shifting himself around some. "Might just be my last one, Tweed."

The two men got quiet for a few minutes, Tweed watching and tending to the fire, taking fresh hot coffee from Cookie.

"You know, never having kids has been bothering me," the old man finally said. "You're the ranch manager. Tweed, how'd you like to own my spread? You might as well be my son, been with me all these years, puttin' up with all my gettin' in the way. When we go back, let's see if we can put that together."

Tweed sat silent, misty-eyed, unable to say a word. Sam finally got up and sauntered into his tent.

"Won't be hard to do that," called out the rancher through tent flaps. "You're already in my will."

* * *

"Morning already?" Sam said, trying to get unsnarled from his bedroll. "What happened to sleep time on this drive?"

The camp was alive with movement. Tweed was standing at the teepee entrance with coffee in hand for the boss.

"Can't be morning already," snarled the boss, fighting with his boots.

"Cookie said you were snoring so loud last night you darn near spooked the herd," Tweed teased. "Be light in an hour, boss. Beans, bacon, and biscuits are hot and ready, and the crew is raring to go. Roll 'em out, old man."

Sam snorted, grumbled, and coughed, but when he emerged from his tent, he had that Tyson smile across his face.

"Must have been like that log we hear about," said Sam. "I'm feelin' good this morning. Muscles sore and tied up, back aching for my old rocker on the porch, and my lips are burned brown from that blazing sun yesterday. Yep, feels good!"

Tweed gave him the rundown on the herd and crew.

"Two streams and lots of rock is the best way to describe today," explained the foreman. "We'll be going a lot slower. Be in the trees tonight and then into high pasture tomorrow."

"Hate to admit it, but I think I need an easier ride today after yesterday," declared Sam. "Wasn't that many years ago I would have spent the summer up here with the herd. Gettin' soft, Tweed, that's what it is. Not old, just gettin' soft." Still chuckling to himself, he caught the stud and brushed him down. "You gettin' soft too, hoss?" he said to his mount, throwing the blanket and saddle up. "We still got some good miles in us, don't we pard?"

The old man watched one of his young hands work to get his horse saddled and felt the anger rise when he saw the cowboy smash a fist into the mustang's nose.

"Tweed, bring that boy over here. He needs to have a chat with me."

Sam held the reins of the stud as Tweed brought the cowhand to him.

"You're new on my ranch, son. Don't think we've been properly introduced. My name's Sam Tyson, boss; what's yours?"

Tweed smiled, knowing he'd heard this conversation before.

"They call me Smiley, boss. Smiley Rafferty," and he stuck a big hand out to Tyson.

"Well, Smiley Rafferty," Sam said, shaking the young buckaroo's hand, "there's a few things you need to know to work here. Them old cows out there are the only reason you're on this drive, and the only reason you get paid, and you only have one tool to work them old cows with. Want to guess what that tool is?"

"I guess it would be me," the young man said, just a little proud.

"No, son, not you. That fine-looking horse you just smacked. You wreck or ruin the best and only tool you have, you can't do much work, and would be out of a job. I ever see you mistreat another horse, and you'll be packin' out. Got it?"

The cowboy stiffened, took a deep breath knowing that he was almost fired.

"Yes sir," said the young hand to his boss. Then he nodded at Tweed who was standing there with a grim look. Rafferty got on his cow pony, and rode toward the herd.

Sam mounted and walked the horse toward where the cattle were bedded. Then he turned and watched the sky blaze its way into daylight.

"Don't think that boy'll do something dumb like that again, eh, Tweed?" Sam smiled, nudging the big stud along.

A cold wind kicked up for a few minutes, and the chill felt good wafting across the rancher's craggy face.

"Just look at them colors, old fellow," he said to his horse. "Have to tell Tweed to keep his eyes open for thunderstorms later today. A mornin' breeze like this and colors like them, I can smell rain."

Sam was working the left side of the herd as they started out, Tweed way up front and Cookie way in the back. Couger Jack, an Indian ranch hand, saw Sam ride up and said what the old man had just mumbled to his hoss.

"Thunder today, boss. I can smell it."

"Me too, Jack. When it hits, keep the herd in close. We don't need to hurt any of them, or us." He laughed, saying it. "Member when they had to drag the three of us off this mountain, Jack? Herd bolted, horses spooked, and lightning struck Cookie's chuck wagon. Busted ribs, legs, arms, horses down for good, and many cows and calves hurt. That was a mess, Jack."

"My arm still pains me thinking about it, boss. By the way, Jake trailed out early this morning. Hopes to find a nice big buck for supper tonight."

"Now you're talking, Jack. Get on up to the lead and tell Tweed about the possible thunder. We'll be crossing a couple of creeks, so we want to have everyone prepared. Fresh venison for supper. Yes, sir, now you're talking."

Sam watched the Indian hand lope off to find Tweed. The crew saw the clouds begin to boil and build all morning, and it was early afternoon when the first rumbles of thunder echoed down the mountainsides. The cattle fidgeted and got spooky.

Some of the horses became more difficult to control, and Tweed had the crew as prepared as possible for whatever might happen. He rode up to Sam Tyson, grim-faced.

"Best to hold 'em up, boss. This looks to be a real gully washer coming down on us."

"Give the word, Tweed," said Sam. "Put most of the crew on the herd to hold 'em and plan on keeping them here all night. Change 'em out every few hours so everybody stays sharp and ready. Do you think Cookie's got enough wood to keep a fire going?"

"He's all set. You've got some really good camp boys this year, Sam."

The foreman rode off to have his cowhands hold the herd.

Lightning began blasting the mountains like an artillery barrage, the thunder rolled constantly. The herd bawled almost as loud as the thunder and got more anxious with every bolt of lightning. The electric smell and taste was in everybody's mouth.

Sam Tyson had been in situations like this hundreds of times and didn't think twice about what to do. Walking his horse very slowly, he worked his way back and forth across what he considered his flank, the area where the herd needed protection. It was what every buckaroo on the drive was doing.

Softly singing ballads from his childhood, barroom ballads from other times, even a Christmas carol or two, he and his drovers calmed the herd.

The storm was just about directly overhead when the first drops of cold rain splashed down, building in intensity to an almost blinding squall. A man couldn't see thirty feet. Then the rain turned to hail, heavy large chunks of ice that added to the misery. The herd got louder, and the bawling was followed by more and more movement. The buckaroos had extreme difficulty keeping the cattle in place.

A bolt of lightning crashed into the middle of the bunched cattle. Thunder peeled back and forth off the mountainsides. The cattle broke into full flight in half a second; cowboys spurred their mounts in immediate pursuit, Sam right along with them. Lightning hit all around the herd. Confused, they weren't able to go in any one direction. It took the buckaroos about fifteen minutes before they restored some kind of order. Tweed shouted out orders and men kept their wits about them, saving the herd from disaster.

"Sam, you all right? You hurt?"

"Gol-darn it, Tweed, I think my leg's busted again," said Sam, still in the saddle, his right limb dangling at an odd angle. "Big old cow swiped me pretty hard with a horn as she went by. Get me back to the chuck wagon!"

Cookie used an old trick with rags and kerosene to get his fire going, and it was a raging inferno when Tweed and Tyson rode up.

"Help me get the boss off this horse, Cookie," Tweed yelled, "and have a couple of your boys get his tent up and take care of his horse. He's bad hurt."

They eased him off the stud and laid him on a bedroll next to the fire. Tweed got his chaps off and cut away his pant leg high up on the thigh.

"Got you right in the lower leg, Sam," said Cookie. "Both bones broke all to pieces and coming out through the skin. You really took it this time."

"Tweed," groaned Sam, "Get Cougar Jack over here. He'll know what to do. Darn that thunder! Fetch Jack and then ride back to the herd, Tweed. Cookie, you get to fixin' chuck; these boys are gonna be hungry."

Between the pain, cold, and wet, old Sam Tyson passed out.

* * *

"It's morning, Sam," said the foreman. "I got some hot coffee here for you."

Cougar Jack was kneeling beside the old man in his tent, his long Shoshone face filled with sorrow.

"I had to do something horrible last night, boss," said Jack.

"I know. What did you hit me with?" Sam asked, feeling the lump at the back of his head.

"Just my gun butt, with some leather wrapped around it. I had to, you know that. No man should have to face the pain of losing his leg. I made a nice clean cut, boss, and wrapped and sewed skin over it. Doused everything with whiskey, there shouldn't be any infection. I'm so sorry," and the Indian buckaroo had wet eyes.

Sam Tyson was very quiet. He finally reached out and took Jack's hand.

"Cougar, you've been a good friend, a good hand all these years. You did what you had to do. Now, as I feared when we started this ride, this is definitely my last cattle drive. Have Tweed send a man down to the ranch and bring a wagon up."

Two cowboys rode to the ranch to get the wagon. Cougar Jack stayed with Sam while Tweed and the hands pushed the cattle the last way up to summer grazing. Cookie left plenty of food with the old man, knowing the Indian would take good care of their boss.

"Looks like that old rocker on the front porch is going to get plenty of work," commented Sam Tyson the next day. “Jack, see if you can find a couple of good stout limbs that I can carve for some crutches. I’m not gonna just sit on my skinny behind for the rest of my life. I got work to do around my place.”

Three days later, Tweed and a group of ranch hands rode back to the camp where the old man was still waiting for the wagon.

“Left two men up there for the summer, boss,” said Tweed. “We’ll need to re-supply them every once in awhile. The old line shack stood up to the winter well, and there’s plenty of grass and water.”

“Good to hear,” said Sam.

Two cowhands returned with a wagon. They loaded the old man aboard and slowly made their way back to the home ranch. Sam sat upright telling stories and joking with every cowboy who rode up to see how he was doing. He made the best of it despite the pain. He spent hours carving out crutches on the forked wood Cougar Jack found for him. They were finished by the time they arrived.

“Tweed, I want you to join me on the porch tonight, after supper,” Sam said after they got him in the house and to bed.

It took about two minutes and Sam Tyson was snoring loudly.

“That old man is tough as a rock,” Tweed said to Cougar as they left the bedroom. “I can’t imagine how I would feel if I lost a leg like that. He thinks it's just a new adventure."

"He has the right attitude, Tweed," said Cougar Jack. "We've got a good tough old ranch boss."

* * *

"That's the way to fix a steak, Cookie! Good job!" Sam Tyson said, settling back in his old porch rocker, watching the smiling cook walk away.

The old man lit a big cigar, sipped from a glass of good whiskey, and gently rubbed the stump of his leg.

"Seems to be itching more today, Tweed," said Sam. "Hope that means it's healing. Bumped it once, and dang me, if that didn't hurt."

The rancher settled back, took another long drag on his cigar, and blew smoke at the stars above.

"This ranch has been good to me, Tweed," said Sam, smiling. "Very good."

Then the old man brought out a sheaf of papers he had tucked into the rocker.

"Time for it to be good to you. This is the deed to the property with one little clause. The ranch is yours, lock, stock, and barrel, but I get to keep the house and live here for the rest of my life. Do you go along with that, old friend?" And he handed the papers to his ranch manager.

Tweed once again found himself unable to speak. The foreman stared at his boss through moist eyes. Holding the papers in one hand, Tweed reached out and briefly squeezed the old man's hand. For a long time, not a word was said as the two men sat on the porch watching the big Nevada sky and listening to the late-night sounds. Later, Tweed helped his boss into the house and in to bed.

"This is your home forever, Sam Tyson," said Tweed.

Then the foreman put out the light.

# RAGE ON THE RANGE

"This is the part of my job that I really don't care much for," complained Sheriff Peter Moresby and he spat.

The lawman glared across the room at the two large men, Hans Koenig and Eugene Fairbanks, both bleeding and bruised. Moresby, sheriff of Nye County, Nevada, sat behind his scarred oak desk. The office was in the large courthouse just off the county seat's main street in Belmont.

"You two have been my friends for several years now. Having to put my friends in jail is not something I enjoy. Both of you should be ashamed. I don't know what the judge will say or do, but you two will spend the night back there," he said, jerking his thumb toward the rear of the imposing brick courthouse.

Moresby motioned to one of his deputies. The lawman who had arrested and hauled the men in escorted the two lawbreakers to the back of the building where the cells were located. The detained prisoners scowled at each other.

"That feud my friends are involved in isn't going to go away from a simple night behind bars," he said to his under-sheriff, Mike Simpson. "I'm going to ride out to the Koenig ranch and make sure Gretchen is all right. I really don't like this job sometimes."

Hans Koenig came to the rich and fertile Monitor Valley several years ago and started one of the larger cattle and horse ranches. His successful income came from breeding and training re-mounts for the army, and his beef herds were sold throughout central and eastern Nevada. With his wife Gretchen, he raised three children, two boys and a girl. Gretchen Koenig was straight from the old country. Strikingly beautiful, she had a dazzling personality which is part of what led to the two men being in jail.

Hans Koenig, insanely jealous, believed that Eugene Fairbanks had been making moves on his lovely bride. Fairbanks, known to most as Gino, was the superintendent at one of the major mines in the Belmont district. He was tall, handsome, and had a reputation as a ladies' man. The feud had been building ever since Gretchen was caught in town by a fast-moving blizzard that passed through the valley in January. She was forced to spend the night in the hotel and was known to have had dinner with Gino Fairbanks.

"Looks like we might be in for another winter storm," Simpson said, walking the sheriff out to the livery. "I'll take care of things here if it slams in on us."

"Thanks, Mike. It's about a three-hour ride out there, so I may not be back before dark."

Sheriff Moresby mounted his large stud and rode north into the great Monitor Valley. A building norther began blowing into his face. He was still thinking about the two men and their fight.

*"Koenig,* thought the sheriff, *rode all the way into town early this morning just to confront Fairbanks. Why?"*

Morseby urged his horse into a steady trot. Hours later, the question was still locked in his head. He turned his mount into the Koenig property. The ranch spread along the wide valley's eastern edge, covering several square miles. The cattle and horse ranch slid into the foothills of the high Monitor Range to the east. The sheriff kicked up a small bunch of resting antelope on the ride to the main house. Hungry, he was thinking how nice a haunch of pronghorn would look speared on a spit over an open fire. He licked his lips in the increasing wind.

When he came to the ranch house, the bucolic scene ended immediately. He found ten-year-old Marchella holding her two-year-old brother, sitting in a rocker on the front porch, crying.

"Marchella!" he hollered, jumping from the saddle. "Where's your mama?"

The little girl pointed toward the barn several hundred feet to the east but didn't say anything. Moresby saw bruises and open wounds on the girl's arms and legs. He jumped back on his horse and raced to the barn.

"Gretchen!" he yelled, repeating the call two or three times. Finally, he heard a soft moan from inside one of the stalls stretched along the sides of the building. He tore open a gate and found her. She was lying in a heap of blood-soaked straw, bleeding from several open wounds, two at least that looked like knife cuts. He pulled his Mackinaw off and wrapped it around her.

"Gretchen! What happened? Who did this?"

Her eyes were open but not focusing. Moresby was sure she was just moments from death.

"Gretchen," asked the sheriff urgently, "tell me. Was it Hans? Who?"

She murmured, "Not Hans," and she either passed out or died; he couldn't be exactly sure at that point.

When he carefully picked her up, she didn't weigh more than a hundred pounds, which surprised him. The sheriff carried her back to the house, laid her as gently as he could on her bed, and covered her with a blanket. Marchella followed him, holding the baby.

"Get a fire started," he told the girl, "while I help your mama. If you can, put a large pot of water on to boil. Where's little Junior?"

The girl was still holding her baby brother, Thomas, but six-year-old Hans Junior hadn't been seen. Marchella just stood there, staring at her mother. She did not say a word or move to put her brother down. The sheriff realized she was probably in shock and nudged her out of the bedroom, back to the living room, and took the baby from her grasp.

"Lie down, Marchella," urged the sheriff, who guided her to a couch. He put the baby next to her, found a blanket, and covered both of them. It took him just moments to get a roaring fire going and find a kettle for water. Then, the lawman started searching the house for Junior. The rooms were a disaster. Tables were overturned, and things were thrown about as if someone was searching for something.

"What happened here?" he asked himself, going from one disorderly room to the next.

He couldn't find Junior anywhere in the house, so he pulled the kettle of water from the fireplace hook and carried it into the bedroom to start working on Gretchen. He was too late. Covering her cold body with the blanket, the sheriff returned the kettle to the living room. He found some coffee, made a large pot, took a cup for Marchella, and poured a second for himself. Then he sat down on the edge of the divan near the girl.

"I know this is horrible for you, honey, but you have to be a big girl now and help me. We need to find your brother, and I need to know what happened."

The girl just stared.

"Here," he said, holding out the mug for her, "sip some of this. It's warm and will make you feel better. Try to remember what happened. Your mother told me that your father didn't do this. Who did?"

The sheriff waited for her to answer. He remembered Marchella was a feisty little girl who got into mischief often—not serious trouble, childish stuff, just wanting to have fun. She was also strong and willing to help her parents whenever they asked. The girl finally reached for the cup, took a couple of sips, and tried to look up at the sheriff.

"Is Mama dead?" she asked in a whispery voice.

"I'm sorry, honey. It looks like you and your mama put up a pretty good fight. You know I'm the sheriff. I have to know who did this."

He knew he had to get out of the house soon and search for Junior. More importantly, make sure the assailants weren't still around. Yet, the lawman knew he couldn't up and leave the little girl. Not just yet. On top of that, a major winter storm was sweeping down Monitor Valley. A howling wind was driving snow and ice. If he didn't get them out of there quickly, they would be trapped.

"Mama doesn't let us drink coffee," she said, taking another large drink of the hot stuff. "It doesn't taste very good.".

"Perhaps this will make you feel better," Sheriff Moresby smiled, putting more wood on the fireplace and bringing the coffee pot back to the couch. "Can you talk with me now?" he asked, filling both their mugs with fresh brew.

"Papa left early this morning, saying he had something to do in town, and Junior and I went out to milk the cow and throw feed to the calves and foals. Like we always do. I had a basket of eggs, and Junior had a bucket of milk. We were coming back to the house when Mama came running toward us, screaming."

Marchella shuddered, tears forming again, and she set the coffee down.

"I saw two men chasing Mama. One knocked her around and started beating her. Junior ran away, and I ran to Mama. She was screaming, and then the other man caught me and hit me with fists and kicked me. It was horrible. Then they left, I guess. I don't remember."

Moresby knew she was terrorized but he needed to urge her to remember things she didn't want to.

"Did you recognize either of the men? It's very important."

"I know," she whimpered, wiping her nose with the back of her hand. "The man that beat me up works at the bank in town, but I don't know the other one."

She threw her arms around the sheriff, crying like no ten-year-old had ever cried. Moresby just sat there holding her, rocking back and forth, saying all the soft things a man can say to a little girl who saw her mother attacked.

"I didn't see a lot of horses in the corrals when I rode in," he started to say, and Marchella interrupted him.

"The army came last week and picked up more than one hundred and fifty of the two-year-olds. Papa was so happy because he said we didn't have very much money left. He paid the ranch hands and let everyone go to town."

Some of what she said made sense. The sheriff knew he had to find Junior, bury Gretchen, and get the children to safety.

"It's time to be that big girl now, Marchella. You must leave Thomas here on the couch; he'll be safe and warm. We need to find Junior. It's very important because it's getting colder."

Marchella nodded her head and stood up.

"Can I kiss Mama?" she asked, all but breaking the lawman's heart.

He took the girl by the hand into the bedroom. Marchella kissed her mother and tears streamed down her cheeks.

"Mama is still so pretty," said the child, taking the sheriff by the hand and walking back to the living room. "Papa will need me, so I'm ready to go now, Sheriff."

Leaving the baby under the blanket, the lawman and girl searched for Hans Jr. They found him hiding in the barn, shivering from cold, but safe. Junior was physically fine but never said a word to the sheriff or his sister. Sheriff Moresby decided that digging a grave in frozen ground was too difficult. Instead he wrapped the body in a blanket and took Gretchen to the cold barn, and placed her in a tack room. He said a few words over her and closed the door to keep her body safe. Then he quickly rounded up his stud and started for the house. The youngsters were waiting, safe and warm next to the living room fire.

"Get everybody dressed for a cold ride back to town, Marchella," instructed Morseby. "I'm going to go harness the team and hitch them to the wagon. See if you can put something together to eat for the ride in."

"Yes, Sheriff, I'll do my best," said Marchella.

The lawman quickly rode back to the barn.

"That little girl is going to be fine," he muttered to himself.

He watched huge black clouds tumble across the Toquima Mountains to the west. Driving snow was coming down, the wind was howling, and massive drifts were building.

"This is going to be one cold ride," he told the horses as he harnessed the team.

The sheriff went to the house for the children and they rode out a half hour later. Marchella sat on the seat next to Moresby, and Junior and baby Thomas were in the back, wrapped in bundles of blankets. The sheriff's stud was tied to the wagon's tailgate.

"Junior," said the sheriff, "you make sure you and Thomas are wrapped tight in those blankets. We'll keep right on going, but later we'll have some food to eat."

The lawman gave the two older children a big smile, trying to assure them everything would be fine but not necessarily believing it himself. The storm howled and screamed its fury, snow so thick and blowing that Moresby sometimes could not see the trail in front of him. He had to look down to the wagon's side to ensure they were still on the road. An hour later, Marchella gave Hans food and water and the baby milk. Then she made sure her brothers were warmly wrapped. The blowing wind was so noisy that it was useless to even think about talking. It was a miracle the two horses could pull the wagon through the increasing snow drifts.

It was late night when they arrived in town. They suffered from nothing more than simply being cold and miserable. Moresby drove the team straight to the courthouse and tied it off.

“I was really getting worried, Sheriff,” Mike Simpson said, coming out to help. “Where’s Gretchen?”

“Let’s get the kids settled first, Mike. There’s been terrible trouble,” he said, lifting Hans Junior and baby Thomas out of the wagon while Simpson gave Marchella a hand. “Go in the office, children, and stay by the big wood stove. We’ll be in shortly.”

He opened the courthouse door for them and handed the toddler to Marchella.

“There’s big trouble right here in town, Sheriff,” Simpson said, pulling a couple of baskets out of the wagon. “Three men, all masked and holding shotguns, robbed the bank, killing old man Tattersol, and then robbed the saloon and gambling hall, killing two more men.

“They rode south, but I called off the chase after a couple of hours. The blowing snow made it impossible to track them.” Simpson fumbled with the baskets. “I couldn’t do much else.”

“I know who one of those men is,” Sheriff Moresby said and spent the next ten minutes bringing his deputy up to date. “If Hans Koenig had that horse sale money at his place, then those men now have many thousands of dollars with them. They most likely hit the ranch right after Hans was arrested and then came directly back here. They went to robbin' the town after I left."

The sheriff in anger and frustration slammed his fist into the side of the wagon, skinning his knuckles raw.

"Hans should never have left his wife and family unprotected," exclaimed Moresby. "Gretchen's death is in part because of that man's unreasonable jealousy."

"It sure is a tragic outcome, boss," replied Mike Simpson.

"All right," said the sheriff, "I'll take the wagon and horses to the livery. You stay here. Then we'll get the children settled at the hotel and someone to watch them. I'm going to have one hell of a lecture for Hans Koenig. Some of this never would have happened if he had been home where he belonged."

* * *

Drifts deeper than most men are tall filled all the gullies and ditches, giving the appearance of a flat landscape as the sun sparkled down on Belmont the following morning.

"Might have been two feet of snow if it had come straight down instead of blowing through here horizontal like," Simpson said, coming into the office. "You have a talk with Koenig?"

“One beat up and crushed rancher this morning,” said the sheriff. “I told him I should charge him with something for leaving his family alone with all that horse money. He was a fool for being upset over Fairbanks having supper with his wife. But I did get some good information on the men responsible.”

The sheriff poured a cup of coffee for himself and one for Simpson.

“Last night, Marchella described the other hold-up men who were with banker Jackson,” continued Moresby, “I told Hans, and he said they were the ones from the army. They paid him and rounded up the horses and left. I figure when they saw Koenig get arrested for fighting Fairbanks, greed drove those men to act. The storm was an accidental break for those killers.”

Sheriff Moresby rocked back in his chair, sucked some more coffee down, and continued.

“I don’t know how many times I can say it, but robbing Koenig’s ranch all boils down to Han’s stupid rage and to allowing all of his ranch hands leave to go to town.”

It was very quiet in the office for several minutes. The two men sipped coffee and shook their heads, absorbing what Moresby said.

“I need you to go to the army post and give a full report,” the sheriff said to Simpson. “Those killers and thieves are well out of this area now, so all we can do is put up posters that they are wanted men."

"What do we do about Koenig and Gino Fairbanks?" asked Simpson.

"Let them go," responded the sheriff. "Koenig's responsible for his wife's death, but his punishment is that he realizes it. Every time he looks at his children, he'll remember why they don't have a mother. He'll live with that act of foolish rage every day for the rest of his life."

# THE ORIGINAL WYOMING KID

"My name's Wyoming, sister. I'm the original Wyoming Kid, so don't give me no lip," he said, slamming a gold coin onto the bar. "I want a shot of whiskey, 'bout three fingers worth, and a good cigar. So get to it."

"Pick up your gold, cowboy, and get out. I don't serve rowdies, and I don't serve little boys. Right now, you're too young to drink, and you've already got a bad attitude. So you ain't drinking. Grab leather or get out."

She reached under her side of the bar and came up with a monster of a double-barrel shotgun. Its diameter made it probably a ten gauge, or maybe even an eight—what the market duck hunters use, a punt gun. The cowboy, no more than sixteen at best, swore under his breath. He picked up the twenty-dollar gold piece and slowly backed out the double doors and onto the dusty street. The self-proclaimed Wyoming Kid had ridden in just five minutes ago, and now he was being chased out. It was by a mad woman saloon owner with a shotgun the size of a canon.

"Perkins, Nebraska," the Kid remembered seeing the name on a wooden plank as he rode into town. "Don't think I much like this town."

Being thrown out of a saloon wasn't new to this so-called Original Wyoming Kid. He started out in life as John Peter Holcomb. Having read every issue of every magazine ever published that featured stories about Western bad men and gunslingers, he took up the name of the Wyoming Kid. When he was younger, he told a little ten-year-old girl his new name, and she couldn't stop giggling for hours. Ever since, he hated girls and women.

"She mocked me!" said the Wyoming kid under his breath and went on, complaining loudly. "A stinking two-bit town with a two-bit saloon owned by a woman! She dares to throw the Wyoming Kid out? Maybe I'll just burn this place to the ground."

The street measured some three hundred feet. In his vision were another saloon, a gun shop, a hardware that sold farm and ranch equipment, and a barber shop that doubled as a dentist's office and offered hot baths for twenty-five cents. That was on the north side of the street.

All the buildings facing south got the sun in their front doors. On that south side were the livery stables, a blacksmith shop, and a pen for the sale of cattle, sheep, and horses. The back side of those businesses faced the railroad tracks, with built-in loading chutes.

"Don't see one animal in them pens," mumbled the Wyoming Kid. "When I rode 'cross them tracks, they was rusty. Some town this is."

The Kid pulled his horse from under the lone tree, mounted, and rode down the dusty street to the other saloon. He tied his tired stud off and walked in for his three fingers of whiskey and a good cigar.

"What the heck is this?" complained the Wyoming Kid to the woman behind the bar. "Didn't I just see you up the street?"

"No, you didn't, cowboy, that was my sister. But if you already saw her and now you're down here, it means she throwed your skinny butt out. So, don't expect nothing. You ain't gettin' any more here than you got there, Kid!"

Like her sister, the lady barkeep took no chances with the pistol-packing Kid. The woman pulled another large double-barreled shotgun out from under the bar.

"Pack it in and back out. You ain't drinking or causing no trouble. Git."

The Original Wyoming Kid found himself once again slowly backing out of a saloon at the behest of a massive piece of firepower.

"I just don't much care for this town," the Kid muttered once again.

Going to his horse, he stepped into the stirrups and began to ride out of Perkins, Nebraska. It hadn't dawned on the boy yet, but the only two people he had seen since riding into town were the sisterhood of saloon keepers.

"Wonder how far it is to the next town. Maybe the blacksmith can tell me," he said, wheeling the stud toward the sale yard.

That stiff, cold wind that can be found often in the prairie country blew great bundles of tumbleweed down the street amid billowing clouds of dust. It mixed with who-knows-what, hammering the boy and his horse.

"Nope, I don't think I much care for this town," became a repeated chorus from the boy's lips.

The planks and posts of the holding pens and loading chutes of the Perkins Sale Yard, Livery and Blacksmith Shop were as weathered as the face of the old man who greeted the Kid. The lad looked down at him from his hoss.

"Doesn't seem you're very welcome in them saloons," he drawled.

The blacksmith-livery man gnawed on the stem of a pipe that hadn't tasted tobacco in a long time.

"You looking for work, cowboy? If so, you ain't gonna be welcome here either. Cuz I ain't got no job for rowdy kids that drink and get in trouble. Might just as well git back on that worn-out cayuse and head on down the road."

The old man was standing just inside the open door of the sales yard office. He spit some horrible-looking stuff out into the dust, then stared the Original Wyoming Kid down.

"Maybe I'll just shoot you, old man. Don't like people talking to me that way. You folks in this dried-up pitiful burg act awfully big."

The Wyoming Kid started to reach for his revolver resting in its holster.

"No, you don't, sonny," said the stockman.

Once again, the Kid was staring into massive twin shotgun barrels leveled at his torso.

"My granddaughters don't want you, and boy, neither do I! You git while you can."

The stock agent's eyes narrowed to slits. The kid watched the man cock both barrels of the ten-gauge shotgun. The wrinkled old man's finger twitched. The Original Wyoming Kid did the only smart thing he could. He left.

The Kid rode to the very edge of the town. He looked across miles of open prairie and watched grasses doing the Sabre Dance in the wild Nebraska wind. The boy contemplated his sad life.

"Ain't the way *Leslies* told the story of a Western bad man," mumbled the Kid.

*Leslies Illustrated Newspaper* was almost a bible to the boy during his growing-up years.

"Two women and an old man pulled guns on me today, and none of them got shot. I never even pulled iron."

The Kid nudged his old stud into a faster walk. He saw a line of willows a few miles up the trail and figured on spending the night there.

"Might be water, know there'll be grass. If I can make my flint work, I'll have a fire."

The Wyoming Kid was as low as a sixteen-year-old can get, particularly as low as a sixteen-year-old Western bad man can get.

* * *

"About fifty years back, you build a fire like that, and you'd be a dead man," said a deep voice out of the darkness.

"Who is that?" said the kid, greatly startled. "Where did you come from?"

The Kid jumped to his feet, reached for his hog leg, and remembered it was in his belt hanging on his saddle, some ten feet away.

A man stepped out of the shadows into the light of a large campfire.

"Been eyeing you up for the last five minutes," said the stranger. "Boy, you got no sense of where you are, do you? I saw that fire from a mile down the trail. Back in the day this was Sioux country, Red Cloud and that bunch would have you dead right now."

The strange fellow with the deep voice was tall and skinny. He was dressed in batwing chaps, a heavy shirt, coat, and a big revolver tucked away in a holster. He wore it high on his waist, not low like a gunslinger.

The fellow poured himself a cup of the boy's coffee and then hunkered down away from the fire. He pushed his sombrero back a bit and gave the young fellow a glare that would kill a bull buffalo.

"What you doin' out here all by yourself, boy? You run away from home? Your Ma know where you are?"

"I'm old enough to be anywhere I want to be. A fellow should ask before taking another man's coffee."

That's all the Kid could think to say. The stranger broke into some light snickers, making the Kid even more angry. The lad started to back toward his saddle. The cowboy pulled his weapon, wiggled it a bit, and the boy kneeled back down at the fire.

"You got a lot of anger in those bones, boy. Better be careful who you get riled at. You trying to give the impression that you're a bad man? A big, tough old gunslinger? Cuz, friend, you ain't."

The Westerner slurped the rest of the coffee and tucked his pistol back in its holster. From his coat he found a cheroot, lit it from a burning twig, and continued just looking at the boy.

"I am the Original Wyoming Kid," the youngster blurted out. He started to say something else but was interrupted by heavy laughter. "Don't laugh at me!" the Kid said, his fists doubled, his shoulders set to throw a punch. "You got no right."

"I got all the right I need," the older man said, patting his holster and chuckling at the boy's antics. "You about sixteen? You ain't never gonna see seventeen with that attitude. Why you like this?" Smoke curled through slightly parted lips. Lips wearing a smile. Then the man chuckled again. "The Original Wyoming Kid, eh? Sounds like something out of *Leslie's Illustrated*."

"You darn right it is," said the kid. "I'm mean and fast on the draw. I'm going to make a name for myself."

"Yup, you ain't gonna make seventeen," said the stranger.

He got up, walked over to the boy, grabbed him by his coat front, and jerked him to his feet. Then, the man slapped the kid hard across the side of his head. It knocked the boy back several feet, and he fell onto his rump. The stranger reached down and roughly pulled him to his feet. Then, the older man punched him square on the nose. It brought gushes of blood to the surface. Another heavy slap was delivered across the side of the lad's face. The Original Wyoming Kid stood there crying. The stranger pulled his revolver and pointed it at the kid's head. He lifted the barrel a couple of inches, fired the pistol, and the boy screamed in terror.

"You still want to be a bad man, boy? Get up, sit by the fire, pull your bandanna, and stop that bleeding. And quit your blubbering. We're gonna have a talk, kid—a nice long chat about life."

The man slipped his pistol back into the leather. He grabbed a cup and poured more coffee.

"Come here, boy. Sit a spell with this old-timer. A fellow who can tell what being a bad man is really about."

* * *

"Sun's up, Kid. Get those skinny bones out of those blankets and get a fire going. Move now!"

The older man nudged the boy with his boot. He walked to his horse and took him to a nearby creek for a drink. He returned with an armful of dry willow branches and stacked them next to the fire.

"You almost killed me last night, mister," protested the Kid.

"That's what happens when you spit an attitude at a real bad man, son. You still want to be one?"

"No, I don't. I've never been that scared. Were you telling the truth last night about them killings, knife fights, and all that? Or were you just trying to scare me?"

"I wasn't trying. I did scare you. And yeah, every word I said was the truth. You got it in you to be good, son? Stuff that attitude in a hole somewhere, and you might just make seventeen after all. This is the West, and that bad behavior of yours will get you killed. You never did tell me where home is."

"Several hundred miles east. I ran away weeks ago."

"As you said, two women and a dried-up old stockyard boss pulled down on you since then. And last night," laughed the stranger, "an old gunslinger.

It's time for the Original Wyoming Kid to retire and learn how to survive in the West. Teach yourself how to rope a cow, plow a furrow, or even someday find a wife."

The stranger saddled his horse and stepped into the stirrups.

"Bury that attitude, boy, and live a good life. On the way home, I think I'd skirt around Perkins if I was you," and the old gunslinger laughed long and hard.

The older man waved at the boy and headed out onto the prairie. The lad watched him until the tough fellow disappeared over a hill.

"No," the Original Wyoming Kid said to himself, waving absently at the stranger. "I think I'm going to go into Perkins and apologize for being so young and stupid."

The Kid rode into town about noon. He tied the poor old stud to a dried-up tree and walked gingerly into the saloon.

"Not again! I told you yesterday, no!" and the owner reached under the bar.

The lad was not wearing his gun belt, and he held his hands high and away from his body.

"I come to apologize, ma'am," he said, standing inside the door. "I was a fool yesterday, and now I know that."

"Well, I'll be," said the lady, putting the shotgun back. "It takes a real man to say something like that, and real men are allowed to drink in this saloon."

She pulled out a glass and grabbed a bottle.

"No, I have another confession. I've never had a drink," the Kid said. "My folks don't drink, and I've never tasted whiskey."

"Then I have just the thing for you," said the lady, putting the whiskey bottle back. She pulled another bottle out from under the bar, and poured. "Taste this, Original Wyoming Kid," she said, plunking the glass in front of the boy.

"That's good," he said, taking a second drink. "Is this whiskey? I like it."

"No, that's my special sarsaparilla. You stick with that and your new attitude, and you can drink in here anytime you want."

* * *

"You're a good worker, boy. I'm glad my granddaughter got you all squared away," said the old stockman. "An agent came through yesterday and said the trains would be running next month, and we got a herd coming in about then, too. Get them chutes and fences all mended up, put that poor old stud out to pasture, and I'll get a good cow horse for you. I'll make you my yard manager for as long as you pull your weight. A dollar a day, boy, and a bed to sleep in."

The Original Wyoming Kid muttered to himself, walking out to the corrals, "I think I kinda like this old town."

# THREE-FINGER JACK

It ended with the singular blast from the muzzle of a Colt. The body flung backward with force, clattered through chairs and tables, and thumped on the barroom floor. Blood poured onto the rough boards. The silence that followed felt like an eternity but abruptly ended with the jostling of men and women making for the swinging doors. The rest of the patrons went out open windows or up the staircase with no thought for the safety of others.

Three-finger Jack found himself alone, except for the bar owner and the dead man. He stood quietly at the long oaken bar, wondering if anything had been gained.

* * *

A miner by trade, the name Three-Fingered Jack came from a miscue while crimping a fuse into a blasting cap. It blew two of his fingers into the tiniest of pieces. Jack stood taller than most in his profession. About six feet and two inches tall, with broad, heavy shoulders from heaving an eight-pound double jack hammer every working day for more than ten years. Jack was always impressive at first sight.

He hadn't seen a barber for years, and bathing water was scarce at the mine. He would be lost in a social setting filled with linen, fine china, and silver. On first meeting, most remembered him for the size of his hands and the length of his remaining fingers—hands so large they could pick up about anything without needing a handle. Yet, he had a reputation for being quiet and gentle. Men were fearful, certain ladies grateful.

It was his habit to come to Pritchart Hole every other Saturday to meet with the banker to trade gold for cash. Then, he would buy supplies needed for the next fortnight, go to the saloon, and have a small taste of whiskey. There, he often joined in the singing of a song or the telling of a tall tale. Both of which he was very good at. Three-Fingered Jack had a voice that stopped stampedes. It could carry to the far reaches of Hades. A deep, rich voice, clear as Mrs. Pettigrew's crystal service and sweet as Cuba's finest cane. Sweet Betsy From Pike never sounded better. It was that morning Three-Finger Jack arrived in town before the noon bell and visited with banker Swenson.

"Ahhh, Jack, it's good to see you again. Your account is growing nicely. Have you plans to buy more land around Pritchart Hole?"

Few knew the extent of the vein Jack had been working on for the last five years. Swenson knew by the amount of money that was deposited. The banker had led Jack into some fine land deals; thus, the big miner now had extensive holdings in and near Pritchart Hole. He could soon consolidate his land, build a large ranch, and live a much easier life if he wished. But, for the moment, an easier life of ranching was not part of his desires. It was not in his character to avoid the hard, dangerous work of mining.

Character, that was a trait that was dear to Jack. To Jack, a miner's character was determined by many things. Honesty and strength—morality and manners were part of it. With such a man, his word should never be questioned. Miners underground put their lives in each other's hands. It is a level of trust unknown by those working on the surface.

He looked at the banker and smiled that big-faced smile.

"No, for the moment, I will continue what I do best."

Jack took his tally sheets, gave them a complete and careful scan, thanked the banker, and left. He walked to the general store and spent considerable money on supplies for the next two weeks. The big miner had two men working his claim. He worked underground with them, and those valuable years of trust went both ways. The two miners he worked with were his best and most loyal friends.

"Those mules will be pulling a big load going home, Jack," laughed Joshua, the storekeeper. "You 'bout bought me out."

"It's a long eight miles up that trail, Joshua, but they're used to doing a lot heavier work than that."

Jack put the wagon, supplies, and mules in the shade under the giant oak tree that dominates the center of the little village and stepped into the Pritchart Hole Saloon and Dance Hall for his regular taste of whiskey and a bit of fun.

"Hey, Jack. It must be Saturday," Caleb, the saloon keeper said as Three-Fingered Jack came through the swinging doors.

"Saturday it is, Caleb," replied Jack.

As he sidled up to the long bar, a ruckus was brewing at one of the card tables, and Caleb pointed it out to the tall miner.

“That boy is here to cause trouble, Jack,” said the bartender. “He can’t keep his hands off my working girls. He was caught trying to sneak cards into the deck, and that pistol of his is always under his hand. He looks ready to pull that iron any minute now. One more little thing, and I’m throwin’ him out.”

“You run a clean saloon, Caleb, so holler if you need help. I’ll back your play.”

“I know you will, Jack, I know you will,” replied the saloon owner.

Jack and Caleb went way back to the early days in Austin and then later up in Unionville. Caleb did well with his diggings and saved his money. When the local mines opened at Pritchart Hole, he bought the saloon.

A scream caught everyone’s attention, and heads turned in time to see the young man slap one of the dance hall girls across her face. He knocked her to the floor and was menacing her as she lay there.

“You little tart. When I want a kiss, you kiss me.”

The young troublemaker raised his fist to strike the girl again.

“Hold it right there, fellow,” called out Three-Finger Jack. “You touch that lady again, and I’ll rip your head off.”

Jack had already taken three big steps toward the man when the bad-tempered fellow spun around and pulled his pistol. Jack reached out with a giant hand and grabbed the revolver, giving a mighty twist, breaking two of the man's fingers. Then Jack ripped the weapon away from him. He held the Colt by its barrel and swung the butt into the man's face, driving him clear across the floor and into the bar. Caleb came forward and broke a bottle over the young man's head, which effectively ended the fray.

"You all right, ma'am?" asked Jack, helping the dance hall girl to her feet. She was still crying and shaking from the ordeal. "Perhaps you can go on up to your room, Missy, and get yourself all fixed up."

Jack's smile was genuine, his graciousness typical. The girl smiled hesitantly and then went upstairs.

"Anybody know this fool?" Jack asked pulling the troublemaker to his feet.

The question was followed by silence.

"You're not welcome in this establishment," said the saloon owner.

"Far as I'm concerned," said Three-Fingered Jack to the young man, "you're not welcome in this town. "

Jack, still holding the boy's Colt, pushed the fellow toward the swinging doors and then stopped.

"Look at that, Caleb—he's just a boy!" said Jack grimly. "You keep acting like this, son, and you're going to have a mighty short and ugly life. If I ever see you touch a lady who doesn't want to be touched, I'll have you for breakfast."

Jack moved the boy's Colt from his left hand into his right and was holding it by the handle when the young man, lightning fast, reached in his boot and pulled out a single shot Derringer. As the fool raised the little hide-out gun to fire, Three-Fingered Jack cocked and pulled the trigger of the revolver just once.

* * *

Three-Fingered Jack took his mules and the loaded wagon back to the mine. He told his compatriots what happened and then rode one of the mules back to Pritchart Hole.

"Why are you back in town so soon, Jack?" asked Sheriff John McNabb. "The trial won't be for two days."

McNabb, was a former miner turned lawman. He was short and powerfully built. He rarely wore his side arm knowing most men would rather talk with him than get in a physical confrontation.

"Didn't know if you meant to keep me overnight, John. Didn't want you to think I was hightailing it out of here."

"That's nonsense, Jack. You simply did what every other man in town wanted to do. Shame that boy had to die, though. So young and so stupid. Come on, let's see if we can rustle up a steak over at Gertie's."

There was no room on the board-walk when those two men walked side by side. Massive shoulders and narrow hips filled the walkway.

The sheriff and miner ate a steak supper with mashed potatoes and gravy, topped off with large portions of one of Gertie's apple pies.

"Judge Amos will be in town tomorrow," said Sheriff McNabb. "He might even step up the proceedings if he knows you're already here. I'll talk to him about that. Looks like Caleb has a room for you upstairs over the bar. See you in the morning, Jack."

* * *

A jury of his peers was sworn in, and Circuit Rider Judge Amos Jenkins presided over the court. It was set up in Caleb's saloon, and the proceedings began. Three-Fingered Jack was sworn in.

He was questioned by the town's attorney.

"Yes," Jack said. "I had to shoot the boy because that little Derringer was aimed right at my head. Yes, I took the boy's gun away from him when he threatened to shoot me. Yes, it was a horrible thing to have to kill the boy, but it was purely self-defense. Yes, the boy struck that young lady, and was going to do it again. That's something no decent person would tolerate."

The jury, listening, nodded in agreement with every statement Jack made. Sheriff McNabb was questioned next.

"Three-Fingered Jack did what any righteous man would do," exclaimed the lawman. "As far as smacking the boy, Three-Fingered Jack had every right to defend the lady and himself. And, as far as that goes, also when the boy tried to shoot him."

Again, heads belonging to the jury nodded in approval.

"Well, Jack, what else have you got to say?" Judge Jenkins asked.

Three-Fingered Jack stood up, towering over the assembled court. He was wearing spanking clean work pants, his shirt freshly pressed by the young lady who had been slapped. His beard was trimmed, and his hair brushed.

"Your honor, I'm sorry that boy had to die. Pritchart Hole isn't a big town but it is a good one. If strangers can come here and slap our women around and threaten townspeople with guns, then it won't be a fit place to live."

"Case dismissed!" ordered the judge as he slammed his gavel down hard and smiled.

There were whoops and hollers from the jury box. The judge's table and chair were removed and replaced by poker tables.

"The bar is open!" declared Caleb loudly.

And...for decades after, August fifth was known as Three-Fingered Jack Day in Pritchart Hole.

# OLD TOM'S ROLL OF WIRE

Old Tom Williams, one of the best hands I ever had working for me, had a few quirks that set him apart from others, but none as important as that old roll of wire that went everywhere he went. If he found part of a fence down, that wire ended up being saved. The old man would wind it into a roll.

"Can't have too much wire," he'd say with a lopsided grin.

It seemed everywhere he went, he lugged that wire. A roll of newfangled bob-wire was for fixing the fences; his roll of plain wire was for any emergency that might come up. Tom liked to tell about the time the old wire saved his life. He's telling the truth because I was a part of the ordeal. It happened one day in November, about 1867, I think. It was not too long after the war finally ended, and we all got back to taking care of our farms and families.

"I'm heading for town, Jake," Tom Williams said to me, bringing the team out of the barn. "We are low on everything, and as long as the weather is like this, I'm going in."

"OK, Tom," I said. "Stay out of the saloons, don't be messing with them painted women, and don't forget the coffee this time."

We liked to fun with each other that way. He told me to go jump in the lake. Then he climbed up on the seat and brought the mules around to head out to the main trail to town. I went to the back of the house to split more wood for the coming winter. The weather was beautiful and crisp, with not a cloud in the sky and no wind. I almost envied Tom's pleasant two-hour ride.

By ten o'clock, the wind picked up from the north, cold and strong, and clouds were right behind. By noon, we had a foot of snow on the ground, and it was blowing in with a ferocious howl.

Hours later, I waded out beyond the barn and strained my eyes, trying to see down the dirt road through the blinding snow. Knowing Tom, he would have that old wagon loaded with all the goods it could carry, and he'd have to rest the mules a time or two.

"I sure hope Tom stays in town," I said to Elsie, my wife. "He took the wagon, and I think right now he wishes he had the big sled."

"This is a mean storm, Jake. You have a right to be worryin' about him."

Her scowl told me to be quiet, and I was, like her, afraid for my friend and farm hand. We sat around the old pot-belly in the living room, downed a second pot of coffee, and waited through the afternoon.

"I wonder if he even left town." Elsie exclaimed.

"I'm gonna saddle old Whiskers," I said and slipped into my big Mackinaw and grabbed my gloves. "If he's on the trail, I'll find him. Keep the fires going. I love you, girl."

I headed out for the barn. I was an hour on the trail when I saw Old Tom and his mules coming toward me at a nice strong walk. There was something very different about the wagon. It seemed out of kilter, the load was piled high with a canvas tied around it, and Old Tom was standing up, driving the team.

"Sure glad to see you, boss. I'm cold and tired and beat and ready to give it up," he said in one long breath.

That wagon was a sight, and I finally had to laugh right out loud. "What have you done, Tom?" I moaned between guffaws. The sideboards were off, the slats from the seat were gone, and even though the mules were plodding along, the wheels weren't turning.

"Had to make skids, boss," Tom said. "Just about used up my old bundle of wire."

Tom had wired the sideboards to the wheels and then used the seat slats to stabilize the new skids. Without the sideboards, the load wanted to tumble out of the wagon, so he had everything stacked high with a canvas holding it in place.

"I've had to stop about every half hour or so and re-do them skids. Ain't much of a sleigh, but the alternative was sittin' by the side of the road until I froze to death. Can't go much further, though, boss. I'm chilled to the bone. Sure hated using up all that wire."

I untied a heavy coat from my saddle and handed it to Old Tom, thinking about how many times I chastised that man for carrying that heavy old roll.

"Don't worry, Tom," I said. "We'll get you more wire."

WELLS, FARGO & CO
EXPRESS
WELLS, FARGO & CO
EXPRESS

# FAILURE AT MONTELLO

Hunched by the fire, Terrell O. K. Okane poured some weak coffee into his tin cup, growling and snarling like an un-caged lion about to attack the great white hunter.

"We hit a sheep camp and got nothin'," spat O. K. "We hit a ranch and got nothin'. Doesn't anyone in this country drink coffee or keep money in their pockets?"

O. K. O'Kane, Silas O'Malley, and Sonny Jameson had busted out of Green River, Wyoming's pitiful little jail the week before. They managed to work their way toward the Nevada border, right through Mormon Utah. Before jail time in Wyoming, the three had not known each other, but each knew the others were outlaws. They palavered and came to an agreement to ride together. There had been friction from the first, each determined to be the boss. Each believed he was smarter and faster with a gun.

"They don't drink coffee," said O. K. O'Kane, spitting the last of his tobacco juice into the fire. "Mormons don't drink coffee."

"What is this with you, O. K?" asked Jameson. "You some kind of city feller can't get along without coffee for a few days?"

"What did we bring this dude along for anyway?" interjected O'Malley.

"It's coffee, fellows," said O. K. "A man can't start the day without a decent cup of coffee."

O'Kane had been complaining from the first morning out of jail, and the other two outlaws were getting tired of it. There was a long silence, and then Jameson spoke up. He had been in this wild country for years, knew the lay of the land and where the railroads were located.

"There's a train station about three hours from here," explained Jameson. "They stop and fill their water tanks and load up with wood if needed. There's a regular cabin there for the watchman. Many trains coming through carry a Wells Fargo car, and that's more important than your darn coffee, O.K."

"You been pushin' me ever since Green River, Jameson," O'Kane snarled. "Keep it up, and this here forty-five will put you down."

"Anytime you're fool enough to try, just you go right ahead," said Jameson as he tipped his hat and simply walked away from the skinny Irishman. Then he turned to look at both men. "Those Wells Fargo train cars carry gold, silver, and paper money as well as jewelry. I know cuz I worked for the Central Pacific for two years. We'll pull out of here at sunrise, ride to the Montello train stop, raid the cabin, and wait for the train. One thing for sure is we'll be out of the cold."

Jameson sat down on his saddle blanket and leaned back on his upturned saddle. He lit his last cheroot and looked around the rough camp.

"You just assume the train will stop," said Silas Slim O'Malley. "I've seen them trains whip right through."

Slim was the largest of the three, weighing well over two hundred pounds. He carried his sidearm low on his left hip and seldom used his left hand for anything other than grabbing iron.

"No, Slim, there's a red lantern that the watchman uses to stop the train. It hangs right there on the water tower. Engineers look for it."

O. K. spoke up quickly, wanting to take some of the steam away from Sonny Jameson.

"How will we know if there's a Wells Fargo car on the train? They look different to you, Mr. Central Pacific?"

"Won't matter none, O'Kane," replied Jameson. "For the next few hours, we'll stop a couple trains that come through going in either direction. We'll rob the crews and force them to head on down the tracks. If one of 'em has the Wells Fargo loot, that'll be our special prize."

Jameson had a nasty grin on his face. He taunted O'Kane with his eyes and easy manner, his big hand and long fingers hovering close to a heavy hog-leg strapped low for a quick draw. O'Kane didn't bite.

"We can't stop more than two or three trains before the first one will be missed," added Jameson. "We'll spend one day in Montello, and then we'll move toward Reno, where the pickin's are easier. I lived there, and the banks are loaded."

Having no other plan, the two companions said nothing further. Sunrise found the three in their saddles, moving across the desert toward the water stop. The January winds howled, scattering snow and sleet with every step the horses took, forcing the men to keep their coats tightly wrapped.

"We been in this storm ever since we left Wyoming," Slim O'Malley cussed.

"This is a new one, I think," O'Kane said. "Coming out of the west this time." He remembered he would have been warm, had coffee, even food of a sort if he had remained in that jail in Green River. "I hate winter," he snarled.

O'Kane was from Chicago, where he ran with several urban gangs. The West wasn't in his blood, and he wasn't afraid to tell anyone.

"Winter in Chicago is mighty cold, but there are buildings you can step into and get warm," said O. K. through the snow and howling wind. "Ain't nothing here but sagebrush."

"Quit yer gripin'," Jameson snarled. "Just quit for more than five minutes."

The water tower stood tall in the distance; the three could see cottonwood trees surrounding a small cabin as they neared the stop. Sonny Jameson explained the layout.

"The cabin door is on the track side of the building, so we should be able to walk right up to it without being seen. With this wind, we won't be heard either. If we tie off in those cottonwoods, we can go right in, guns pulled, and take over.

"Since when do you give the orders?" O'Kane growled.

"Since I'm the one what knows what's goin' on, mister. If you don't want to be in on this, then just ride off, Irishman," Jameson snickered and added, "Or make a play."

There was silence and O'Kane did nothing. Then the three rode up to the trees, stepped out of their saddles, and tied off the horses.

"Don't see no mounts," said O'Malley. "Maybe ain't nobody here."

"There's smoke comin' out of the chimney," replied Jameson, "someone's here,"

Then he led the way around to the track side of the small building. Jameson pulled his Colt, made sure the others had as well, and slammed his body against the door of the cabin. Startled and frightened, four Chinese road workers jumped to their feet. They managed to slip around the three outlaws and rushed out the open door.

O'Kane shot the last worker in the back. The other Chinese ran faster and disappeared down an arroyo.

"What kind of fool move you makin'?" yelled O'Malley. "There was no reason to kill that man! You're a fool, O'Kane."

It wasn't just the small cabin that made things feel mighty close. Both Jameson and O'Kane still held their weapons, glaring at each other.

"Looks like there's coffee and food, boys, and a warm stove to stand next to," said O'Malley. "You two go ahead and shoot each other; I'm gonna make another pot of coffee."

O'Kane moved first, slipping his pistol into his holster and walking toward the stove. Jameson just smiled and walked out the door to make sure the Chinese worker was dead. Then he dragged the body into the brush.

* * *

"Looks like they're making for Nevada, Sheriff," Stony Welles said.

The three lawmen walked their horses into a cold camp not too far from the banks of the Great Salt Lake. Green River sheriff, Emory Smith, got down from his horse, knelt, and checked for heat. Then he ran his fingers through the cold fire pit. Once again, he settled back onto his saddle.

"Afraid you're right, Stony, that fire's cold. They're about a day ahead of us now, so let's put these ponies into a nice long trot and catch up."

Sheriff Smith, his deputies Stony Welles and Warren Culbertson, moved out fast, following the three escapees as best they could through the deepening snow.

"They don't seem to be covering their trail," Stony said. "Course, listenin' to that fool O'Kane might have changed the other two outlaws' judgment."

The three lawmen got a good laugh out of that.

"Sheriff, they probably figured that you wouldn't go outside your jurisdiction to find them," said Culbertson.

"When we catch up," said Sheriff Smith, "we want to be very careful of Sonny Jameson. He's a wanted killer, escaped from Leavenworth, and has two lawmen notched on the handle of his Colt. O'Kane is a loud-mouthed idiot, and the only danger from Slim O'Malley is that he can pick you up and crush you with his bare arms."

"O'Malley is a dullard, and I'm sure Jameson already has him in line," said Culbertson. "I figure O'Kane will get Jameson riled at every opportunity until Jameson puts him down permanent."

It was early morning when they found another fire pit. The sheriff got down and checked it with a stick and found warm coals. He had a slight smile on his face.

"They're not moving as fast as they were. They left here this morning. Let's ride hard, and we'll have them outlaws by this afternoon."

"I don't know why, but it looks like they're headin' deep into Nevada" said Stoney Welles. "They tried to rob those ranches and got nothing, and now they look to be headin' where there ain't any people."

"You're right, Stony," the sheriff said, "but there are railroad tracks. Ain't never been in this country, but I know the railroad that runs through Green River comes through here somewhere. Let's just stay hard on their trail, boys."

* * *

"You got that lantern lit, O'Kane?" asked Jameson.

"Yeah, and hangin' on the hook. You sure this will actually stop the train?"

"It will."

O'Kane just stared at Jameson and then walked back into the shack for another cup of hot coffee. O'Malley stood outside next to the station door, smoking. Jameson motioned for him to come away from the building.

"Engineer sees that red lantern, and the brakes are set," said Jameson. "All we have to do is walk out of the shack, guns cocked, and take their money. I don't trust O'Kane much, so I want you to cover the Wells Fargo car."

"You keep pushin' him, Jameson," said O'Malley, "and he'll shoot you sure as I'm standin' here. Let's get out of the cold and have some of that coffee."

As the two men walked through the station door, O'Kane pushed them aside as he rushed to the outhouse. He had wolfed down half a loaf of stale bread he found in a cupboard and felt lucky he got to the necessary building in time. As O'Kane shoved Jameson, the hot tempered outlaw started to reach for his pistol. O'Malley stopped him. "Not now!" he said.

Sonny Jameson and Slim O'Malley seemed to get along fine. Neither one got along with O.K. O'Kane.

"That dead Chinese ain't gonna go over well with the railroad, Slim," said Jameson, finishing his coffee. "I dragged him into the bushes, but can you help me toss the body in that arroyo?"

The two outlaws went out the door and lugged the dead man to the edge of the ravine and threw him in.

"Train comin'!" O. K. hollered as he left the outhouse.

He was still buckling his pants and gunbelt. The outlaws dashed into the cabin and watched as the train with three cars slowly puffed its way into the station. As soon as the heavy steamer was fully halted, the outlaws walked from the shack, guns drawn. Bandannas were pulled up over their noses.

"Good afternoon, Mr. Engineer," said Sonny Jameson as he swaggered up to the engine. "Come on down, bring the fireman, and let's have all your money." He pointed to O'Malley. "Go see if the brakeman is back there, disarm him and bring him up here."

Jameson turned to O'Kane. "Check those boxcars," he said.

The engineer and his fireman climbed down from the pulsing engine, hands held high.

"We don't carry no money," the engineer said.

O'Kane hesitant to follow Jameson's orders, remained where he stood. He slapped the trainman across the side of the head with his revolver.

"Stupid move," Jameson snarled at O'Kane as he helped the engineer to his feet. "Just empty your pockets, old man. You, too," he said, pointing his pistol at the fireman.

Slim O'Malley came back up the tracks, pushing the brakeman ahead of him with the barrel of his gun.

"One boxcar is marked Wells Fargo," said Slim. "Brakeman says it's empty, which means, of course, that it's not."

This was followed by laughter from the three outlaws. Sonny Jameson jerked the brakeman over next to the engineer and fireman.

“Let’s have your money,” said the outlaw leader.

Jameson, O’Malley, and O’Kane herded the train crew into the shack and tied them up before trudging down the tracks to the strongbox on wheels. O’Kane walked right up to the rail car and tried to open the sliding door. Suddenly, it moved about three inches, just enough for a shotgun barrel to be pointed out. The shot blew half the Irishman’s head off, and the door slammed shut again.

“Open that door and give us your strongbox, and you’ll live to see another day,” Jameson yelled.

He was answered by two shots from a revolver, through the walls of the rail car. The two outlaws fired several shots in return and heard a muffled curse from inside.

“Open the doors, fool, or we’ll just keep shooting,” shouted Jameson.

That was answered by two more rounds from inside the boxcar. One nicked Jameson. Jameson cursed and ripped his bandanna from his face and used it to stop the blood leaking from his right forearm.

“Shoot the lock and we’ll get that door open,” yelled O’Malley. Together the two men fired three quick rounds. The car door moved slightly. Slim put his weight and strength into it, nudging it open by a few inches.

"Come out of there with empty hands," ordered Jameson, pulling on the door and making a wider opening.

His command was answered by a shotgun blast that knocked Jameson five feet backwards. It left him with no throat and blank, staring eyes. O'Malley ducked down and slid to the left of the boxcar so any gunfire from inside could not hit him.

"You've had your fun, mister, and now it's time for you to die," said the last remaining outlaw. "You have five seconds to come out of the boxcar or I burn you out."

O'Malley slipped down the tracks and into the sagebrush. He collected tinder and brought it back to the Wells Fargo car. Then he lit some of the brush. It went up in flames and the big outlaw tossed it through the boxcar's open door. Slim waited a moment, lit another branch, and tossed it in. Acrid smoke filled the car and the Wells Fargo agent inside coughed loudly.

"Come out of there, you idiot!" shouted Slim O'Malley. "With your hands empty where I can see them."

It took one more lighted sagebrush branch before the man clambered out of the smoke. Slim waited until he was all the way out, then shot him dead. Climbing inside the boxcar, the big man kicked burning boxes through the wide door. He slapped out the remaining fire with a blanket from the guard's chair. Then he started looking for money and anything else of value.

* * *

"See those trees and the tank? That's the water tower, Sheriff," Stony Welles said, pointing at the Montello Station. "Looks like there's a train."

"If these tracks mean anything, whoever's onboard is in serious danger," Sheriff Smith said, kicking his horse into a gallop. "We better get there before it's too late."

As they came near the station, they spotted three horses tied off in the cottonwood trees. Then they heard a single shot coming from one of the boxcars.

Giving their horses a good kick in the ribs, the three lawmen raced toward the train. They spotted Slim O'Malley climbing into a smoking boxcar. It appeared that he did not see or hear them approaching. The sheriff and his two deputies dismounted beside the train. The lawmen drew their pistols. Sheriff Smith spotted three bodies on the ground. Two of them were O'Kane and Jameson.

"It's over, O'Malley!" called out the sheriff. "Leave your weapons and climb down out of there."

The lawman motioned his deputies to stand to the side of the boxcars. O'Malley's gunfire from inside the Wells Fargo car splintered wood.

"One last chance, Slim," the sheriff hollered. "Easier for us if we just bury you here. Come out of there!" He gave the big outlaw inside another few seconds to make up his mind.

"Time's up, Slim!" announced the sheriff and he emptied his pistol into the boxcar. Culbertson and Stony Welles did the same thing. After the smoke cleared, the three waited. There was complete silence. Sheriff Smith took a chance and stuck his head inside. Then he climbed up into the Wells Fargo boxcar.

"Looks like we got some burying to do, boys," said the sheriff, dragging O'Malley's body towards the door.

Inside the station they freed the train crew. With great difficulty, they broke frozen ground with a pickaxe and buried the outlaws and the Wells Fargo agent.

"All those bodies," said Sheriff Smith, "over a hundred dollars in cash and silver dinnerware destined for a hotel in Chicago."

The three lawmen entered the warm station and joined the train crew. Sheriff Emory Smith sat at the table and sipped hot coffee.

"Times like this, I really don't like my job," he said. "When the train to Green River comes through we'll load all the horses on a boxcar and ride back in comfort. Not one of those fools was worth the life of that Wells Fargo agent or the Chinaman."

Author's note:

This story is roughly based on an episode at the Montello, Nevada water stop. The outlaws didn't do well or survive that attempt, either.

HARDWARE
& MINING SUPPLIES

# THE VALDEZ EVENT

Grady had never been in a situation like this in all his fourteen years. He was afraid on the one hand, anxious to find out what was going to happen on the other. He was well concealed behind a stack of barrels in front of the general store. Some filled with flour, some with whiskey, and some with molasses. In the street, not twenty-five feet from his hiding place, stood the sheriff, Mean John McGinty, angry and looking to kill his man.

Mean John McGinty got his name the old-fashioned way: being mean. He never gave anyone an even break and never went out of his way to help a stranger or even an acquaintance. McGinty was most pleased when he didn't have to arrest someone; instead, he preferred killing them. He'd say, "Saves this county hundreds of dollars a year in court costs and jail time. They're criminals, do 'em in, get rid of vermin."

Grady watched as McGinty put pressure on his latest victim. In other communities, he might be considered a suspect; in Santa Ricardo County, he was a victim. Juan Valdez, a fifth-generation rancher and horseman in Santa Ricardo County, stood straight, eyes bright, shoulders squared, listening to the diatribe coming from Sheriff McGinty.

"Word I have, Valdez, is you've been using a runnin' iron on some of the cattle around here that don't belong to you. Stealin' another man's cattle, it's called rustlin' in case you don't know your English too well, calls for a hangin'."

"My English is better than yours, Sheriff, so don't play the racial game with me. I've never stolen anything in my life, and would never steal another man's cattle. My family has been in this valley for over a century, and that's sure as hades more than you can say."

"You proddin' me, Valdez? I don't take to proddin', boy." McGinty had his right hand hovering near the Colt hanging from a gun belt filled with bullets and covered with silver conchos. "Now you unhook that belt of yourn and turn around so I can put the chains on you."

"I'd rather not do that, Sheriff. I've not done anything wrong. You just want to get rid of me and then take my ranch like you've done others. No, I think you'll have to take my guns away from me in a fair fight, sir. I'll not give in to your devious ways, McGinty."

Grady, the boy, had never seen anything like this, a man standing up to Mean John McGinty? He found that he was holding his breath for so long that he got dizzy. Juan Valdez was a friend of Grady's family; in fact, he was a friend to most of the people in the valley. Were there others watching? If not, Grady would be in danger himself if McGinty killed Valdez, and he was the only witness.

At holidays, special events, and fiestas, the Valdez family often supplied large amounts of food and drink, always provided entertainment by way of Mexican bands and dancers, and showered brides and grooms of the various families with gifts and money. He was a stable and willing member of the community. It was his very successful ranch that brought about this confrontation on the main street of Santa Ricardo.

Sometime around the mid-1700s, the Spanish crown created a large section of land in a valley north of what is now the Mexican border. With the border change, it eventually became part of the United States. The land grant was given to Victorino Valdez for special services rendered to the crown. Most of the grant remained in the Valdez family up to this day. The other various sections pealed off to married sons and daughters over the last hundred years.

Along with raising some of the best cattle in the area, the Juan Valdez ranch provided squash, beans, corn, fresh fruit, and hay to local merchants. It was well-known that Mean John McGinty was a greedy fool and had designs on Juan's ranch.

Grady wanted to get out of his hiding place and run for home, but if he moved, the sheriff would see him. The lad had already heard and seen too much. He may only be fourteen, but he was wise. Grady hunched down further behind the group of barrels. If this was two hours later, or any other day besides Sunday, there would be people all over the street. But right now, there were only three: the sheriff, the victim, and the witness.

Grady was in town because of his mother's egg business. Sunday morning activities started before daylight. It involved delivering eggs from his mother's hen house to half a dozen homes up and down the streets. She insisted that her customers have their eggs early. Following deliveries, Grady usually raced home to milk the goats and old Bessie, their cow. But when he saw the sheriff approach Valdez, he ducked behind the barrels.

"I'm giving you one last chance, here, Valdez. Drop that gun belt or die."

"You aren't going to kill me like you have many others, McGinty. It won't be that easy. I'm younger and far faster. You like the idea of killing a man when there are no witnesses, don't you? How do you know I don't have my charros with me? See, you're already looking around. Do you find them, Sheriff? You're a blowhard and a fake. You shoot people in the back. Come on, then, let's see if you're good enough. I've committed no crime. You have no right to challenge me."

Mean John McGinty hadn't been talked to in this manner, ever. His intimidating demeanor was usually enough to make his victims back down. Something had gone wrong; he underestimated the rancher. He had spent years coveting the Valdez ranch, and this moment was his opportunity. All he had to do was kill the Mexican, wait for the county to put the property up for bid, and take it by intimidation.

McGinty looked around once more. It was sunrise and there were no people on the street. He stared Valdez in the eye and moved his big body closer. To frighten victims was his way, and McGinty frightened people. His eyes narrowed, his mouth was grim, and his hand near the butt of his pistol—nerves ready for the draw. How many times had he cocked the hammer and cleared leather? It's so easy to pull the trigger and stand over his victim and watch him bleed out.

"I'm waiting, Valdez."

McGinty did not know that Juan Valdez had fought Indians, rustlers, and bandits. The rancher had killed men when necessary and he was fully prepared to defend himself this morning. He saw McGinty look around once more, and then the sheriff's right arm and hand jerked at his pistol butt. Juan reached for his Colt just as McGinty said, "Valdez." The sheriff's iron never cleared leather. The heavy chunk of lead from Juan Valdez's pistol tore through the lawman's heart, knocking the man backward. McGinty crumpled lifeless in the dirt.

Slowly, Grady emerged from behind the barrels.

"Where did you come from?" Valdez was surprised by the boy's appearance. "Did you see and hear all of this?"

"Yes, sir, I did. The sheriff was going to kill you, wasn't he?"

"I'm afraid so, Grady. I'm afraid so."

Within minutes, the town's people were on the street. They checked out the body of a man they most feared, talking among themselves. The villagers listened to Valdez and Grady, and agreed the rancher had no choice.

* * *

"I'm so sorry I'm late, mama."

Then Grady explained to his mother what transpired in town.

"I'm back now. I'll take care of the goats and old Bessie right away."

"I never knew you were so brave," said the boy's mother. "How horrible for you to witness that shooting. Come now, I'll help you with the milking."

# COW CAMP MORNING

I guess it's just that, as a morning person, I feel I get to enjoy so much more of what this world offers, daily. Some find it a drudge to clamber out from that warm bedroll in time to witness the start of a new day, but I never felt like that.

To hear the birds burst forth their songs of welcome, to feel the surge as the coldest part of the day happens and then begins to warm when old man Sol makes his appearance, becomes a delightful stab of pleasure.

Yes, sir, winter mornings can be difficult until one steps out of the tent. I wake automatically, it seems, about half an hour before the sun actually appears. Slipping from a comfortable bedroll into sub-freezing temperatures can best be described as brisk. Once shirt, pants, and jacket are donned, one warms rapidly, and then watching the day unfold is exhilarating.

Usually, the wind picks up stirring dust devils, creating their own little piece of chaos. To see the eastern skies slowly take on painterly light and color is thrilling. Seeing early mists rise through cold air becomes simply heaven. And across the landscape with the rising sun, dark changes to bright colors. There is a deep blush of purples to the tints and shades of red, tangerine, and yellow, and gradually the sky turns a soft blue.

Horses begin to mill about in the rope corrals. I like to hear the cows bawl for their calves. Old Cookie grumbles about everything but does it with a broad stroke of pleasure, lighting the cookfires, mixing hot cake batter, and storming about when the camp boys aren't quite right with dry wood. Coffee boils, and its wonderful aroma drifts into the atmosphere. And when Cookie strikes the iron rod to the iron triangle for the first time, it's a pleasure to hear grumbling from every tent as the buckaroos get both legs into pants, feet into boots, arms into shirt sleeves.

The coffee seems so much better in the early morning. The fire feels friendly and warm. And the buckaroo that got chewed out the night before because of how he treated his horse actually smiles and says 'good morning' to you.

Ten minutes before the first light, there was silence. Ten minutes after the sun peaks over that far range, life has exploded, with some young horses putting on their morning rodeo, some heifers storming about because of a 'lost' calf, and even a buckaroo screaming that someone stole one of his boots. Cow Camp at sunrise is an experience no one should miss.

Looking far down the valley, there's the home ranch we left yesterday, the sun just now reaching into those lush pastures. Turning my head the other way, I see range after range, stretched out for a hundred miles. The sun splashes off the peaks, and the deep canyons remain black with night, waiting for the rising joy of light.

Cookie surprises us with great chunks of side meat and plates full of biscuits and gravy for our morning repast. Buckaroos stuff some meat and a couple of biscuits inside their saddle bags for later in the morning. Saddles are thrown on the backs of the best ranch horses in the basin, and it's time for the traditional morning hail.

"Mount up, boys, we got twenty miles to go."

2 + 4 =
6 - 5 =

## MISS SUMMERS' LESSONS

His friends call him Jack, and his mother calls him John-David. His teacher seldom calls him anything because he rarely shows up for school. The boy's father doesn't mind that much for one simple reason. Jack is an only son among his family of eight, about in the middle, and his father, Edgar "Sonny" Collins, wants Jack to remain on the farm.

*That boy gets too much learnin' and the first thing, he'll be off to St. Louis or something,* thought the father. Sonny had never voiced that to his wife or son, but most men around the county felt the same about their young boys.

It was middle of April, planting and plowing time in the valley, and Jack often stayed home to work. When he did go to school, it was on Thursdays and Fridays.

"I want you to stay after school for a few minutes, John-David," said the teacher in front of the class. "I need to discuss a couple of things with you."

Jack's teacher, Miss Linda Summers, was prim as a fresh peach off a young tree and stern as the devil himself. She started teaching at the County School, as it is known, two years ago.

"Nope, can't stay over, ma'am," said Jack. "Pa needs me to get them ditches cleaned out for irrigatin' and gotta trim the horses' hooves, too, cuz we be plowin' later this week."

Many in the class, first through sixth grade, snickered at Jack's comments.

"It will only take ten minutes, John-David. I want you to stay over."

She had that grim reaper's look in her eyes, her lips drawn tight, her brows furrowed deep as black earth at planting time, and Jack scrunched down at his little desk and nodded.

He said "Fine" in a sarcastic manner, and Miss Summers accepted his defeat with a proper smile on her pretty face. It had taken Jack many years to attain the fourth grade, and at fourteen he was the oldest student at County School. When class was dismissed, Miss Summers motioned for Jack to sit in the chair next to her impressive desk. The kids referred to it as the execution chair. Jack stood almost six feet tall and had a deep chest and heavy shoulders. He took great pleasure in lifting things that no other boy in school would even think about.

"Don't be getting' me in trouble with Pa," said Jack, refusing to sit. "I can't stay but a few minutes, or he'll be all over my, ah...rear."

"You watch your mouth, John-David," exclaimed the teacher.

He stood near the desk with his hands in his overall pockets, and wore a blank stare on his face.

"Sit down," she commanded.

Jack did so very slowly. She might think she's the boss, but in the young man's mind, she wasn't.

"Are you planning to work at your father's farm all your life?" she asked in a quieter voice.

"Reckon so, sure. It's a fine farm with wheat and corn, lots of fruit trees, and stuff. What else would I do? Pa said it would probably be mine someday. So, yeah, darned right, I'm gonna stay."

He was fumbling with his fingers, lacing them and unlacing them, staring down at his hands and at the floor—everywhere but at Miss Summers.

"That's my point, John-David. Exactly."

She was sitting in her chair, her back perfectly straight, her left hand on top of the desk, her right in her lap. She actually smiled at the boy.

"How are you going to know what to charge for a bushel of corn when you don't even know how much a bushel is or how to add and subtract very well? Or, if you're planning to buy some property to add to your farm, how will you know whether you're paying a good price or even figuring out how big an acre is or what a quarter section is?"

"That's crazy talk, Miss Summers," he blurted out. "A bushel basket is this big." He rounded his arms to show the size. "And I can pace off an acre. An' 'sides, ain't nobody gonna cheat me."

He got up to head home before Sonny, his father, got really angry at him for being late

"Foolish talk, ma'am," Jack said, getting more upset as he put on a hat and coat. "Foolish talk. Our wagon holds about a hunert bushels of corn, and I know what the price should be. Dog-gone it, Pa is gonna be mad." He ran out of the schoolroom down the well-worn path to home.

*That teacher was talkin' in riddles,* thought Jack, very perplexed. *What the heck was she thinkin'?*

Late, the boy ran up the path. He came to a sliding halt in front of his angry father.

* * *

"Whew, those ditches were full of mud," said Jack, shifting the shovel to his other shoulder. "'Bout broke my back, Pa."

"Don't be gettin' soft on me, Jack," Sonny barked at the boy.

Together, they walked toward the hand pump in front of the old farmhouse.

"Wash up for supper," said the stern father. "After we eat we need to get them horses trimmed out. Hate to say it, but it looks like rain. Don't want that right now. Too much work before plantin', and sure don't want to try plowing in the mud."

"We'd just have to put it off for a week, Pa. That's all."

"That's all? Ain't you learned nothin' around here?"

Sonny whapped the boy across the back of the head so hard it knocked the lad's hat off and dumped him on the ground near the back steps.

The father stormed into the kitchen. It was warm as toast with the big kitchen woodstove cooking great pots of food.

"We're home, ma. I'm starved." said Sonny to his wife. He threw his hat at one of his girls to hang up. He sat down at the table, ready to say blessing. Jack came in fresh-faced, smiling at his mother, and sat beside his oldest sister, Anna. Jack explained what happened at school.

"What did Miss Summers want to talk to you about, Jack?" his younger sister Maybelle asked. "You in trouble again?"

"Ain't in trouble," he answered, looking first at his mother, then at Sonny. He glared at his sister. "She sure does talk stupid for someone who is supposed to be a teacher."

His mother swallowed a fork full of mashed potatoes and asked her son almost the same question as his sister.

"Why were you kept after school?"

To Jack, there was implied danger in that question. He fidgeted, not looking at anyone, keeping a large bite of food inside his mouth for as long as possible before chewing and swallowing.

"She was talkin' to me about acres and bushels and money and all kinds of stupid stuff, like someone is going to cheat me or something. Silly. Just talkin' riddles."

"Well," his mother said, "how big is an acre?"

There was a long silence before the boy answered.

"It's measured just like Pa does; you pace it off," Jack answered. "Pa knows."

"How big is an acre, Sonny?" his wife asked.

'Bout a hunert paces or so in each direction," Sonny answered.

"You didn't get any more schooling than John-David has gotten," his wife admonished her husband.

"For heaven's sake," grumbled Sonny.

She looked at the two and shook her head.

"Husband, John-David, when you purchase ten acres, you should know what you're buying. When you plant corn, you should know how many bushels to expect per acre."

Jack's mother made it clear that she was frustrated at her husband's lack of education and now what her son was sharing.

"If either of you knew your numbers, we might have a better life around here."

"Now, mother," Sonny said, "I ain't never been cheated! We get good money for our corn and wheat, and I know how much land we have."

"I don't think you know what you're talking about, husband!"

The table got quiet as Sunday church.

"I'm going to tell you how big an acre is, Mister Sonny Collins, and then I want you to figure out how many square feet of land we have."

Her jaw was set, her eyes blazed almost as bright as Miss Summers', and nobody at the table moved.

"Now, gentlemen," she glared, first at her husband and then at her son. "A section of land is six hundred and forty acres. Remember that. An acre is 43,560 square feet. John-David, how do you measure for square feet?"

"Darned if I know," he said, then caught himself. "Sorry. I meant to say, I don't know, ma."

"That's better," and the evil eye moved from Jack to Sonny. "Well? How do you measure for square feet?"

"Who cares?" the father snapped and started to get up from the table.

"No, Sonny, you sit back down! We're not through here. You're going to die one day, and John-David or me or the girls are going to inherit this farm. Right now you don't have any idea how many square feet of land we have. You're dealing in numbers every day—all day—and you don't know what they mean. You say you've never been cheated, but how on earth do you know that? If you don't understand math, then you don't know if you were cheated or not."

No one at the table had ever heard their mother talk this way. Not ever.

"Anyone?" Mrs. Collins asked, looking at each family member around the table. "How big is a bushel?"

There was more silence.

"It's four pecks," she said. "How big is a peck?"

Even more silence.

"A peck is eight quarts dry measure. So then, a bushel is eight times four. How big is a bushel?"

Maybelle answered quickly.

"That's thirty-two quarts, right, ma?"

"Is she right, Sonny?"

Silence.

"John-David?"

Again, silence.

"She's right." said the mother and smiled.

Mrs. Collins looked back and forth to Sonny and Jack and finally spoke again.

"Let's eat our supper, and unless you want to go through this every night from now until I get the right answers, you two gentlemen had better learn your numbers. What you don't know, is that I've been talking with Miss Summers, John-David. And husband, I have every suspicion that the last time you sold corn, you were cheated."

* * *

"John-David," Miss Summers called out. "Come to the front of the class."

Jack stood up slowly and lumbered to stand in front of the large desk.

"Class, John-David got all the answers right on his arithmetic test." She handed the tall young man an apple.

The class clapped. A couple of the boys whistled, and Jack turned as red as the insides of a fresh, ripe watermelon.

* * *

"Really, Sonny," the man at the counter said, "it was an accident. I wasn't trying to cheat you; I just transposed a couple of numbers. Here's the balance of what I owe you for that last shipment of corn you brought in. Sorry about that."

# JUSTIN'S HOLE

The trail into Justin's Hole winds down from the craggy peaks of the Elk Range. It towers at some nine thousand feet into the clouds and thin air. From the crest, one can see the Justin River meandering through a long, verdant valley. But the village remains hidden, tucked away in a horseshoe bend named Justin's Hole. Mist spreads through the tall pines and hardwoods lining the river, offering a splendid vision of high mountain existence.

Three men started the long ride down that trail just after first light—a ten-mile trek that would take them most of the day. Along with a riding horse, each man was trailing a pair of fully loaded pack mules. They made this trip every six weeks, come what may, and often faced harsh conditions either coming or going.

The tall man wearing a fur hat and Mackinaw went by the name of Jake Willoughby, the group's boss. Just behind him was James (Moose Nose) Sam the best packer in Alaska who had once been a scout for Kit Carson. Eating the trail dust of both riders rode Dennis Ledgermain, a French Irisher out of Manitoba.

"Lookin' forward to a hot bath, a big chunk of elk, and a pretty girl," said Willoughby, "and in that order."

They forded a small creek running cold and fast.

"One of these days, we have to stop here on one of our trips," continued Willoughby. "They's got to be trout in these pools."

Neither Moose Nose nor Ledgermain answered, mainly because they couldn't hear what their boss was saying. That didn't stop Willoughby from holding his conversation. Crossing the creek, Moose Nose swung low from the saddle and scooped a handful of water, splashing his face, letting some get in his mouth.

"Good water," he said to the rocks and trees surrounding the trail.

Ledgermain was singing, a high tenor so melodic the trees and breezes seemed to respond. His horses were mellowed out by the sweet sounds and never threw a fit—ever.

About noon, some of the villagers started taking furtive glances up the side of Bull Elk Peak. First was the saloon keeper, then the barber-dentist, and then the smithy who ran the blacksmith shop, general supply and feed store. The blacksmith saw the riders and pointed out to his fellow merchants that it would be a couple more hours before the supplies would arrive.

"I need whiskey," Michael the saloon keeper said, spitting a wad of tobacco juice into the dust.

"Sure you do," the smithy said, "and I could use a load of corn, flour, sugar, and coffee for my shelves too. But lookin' up that old mountain ain't gonna get it here any faster."

So, as they did every six weeks, the three merchants went into the saloon and polished off the dregs of the last bottles on the shelf.

Hours later, the three supply traders rode into Justin's Hole.

"Gettin' any color?" Ledgermain asked the first person he saw.

"'Nuff to pay you boys for the run," replied a miner.

"How's the weather been in the valley?" asked Moose Nose Sam.

"Been cold and rainy here for billions of years now," replied another miner, spitting into the mud of Justin's Hole's only street.

"Lost a few lads to the cons," said the first miner. "Consumption is bad when it's always so blastin' wet."

The three packers took their supplies to various merchants along the street. The mules were unloaded in quick order, and fifteen or so businessmen filled their larders and pantries. Now the saloon keeper was all smiles. Each owner beamed his satisfaction.

"Gonna be winter soon," said the saloon keeper. "You boys need to double up the next load, just in case we get snowed in again, like two years ago."

"Already in the plans, Michael," replied Willoughby, impatiently. "Where's Mr. Dodd? We need to get settled up. I want a hot bath, and can you tell me if little Suzie is still in town?"

"Old Clem Dodd went off to the Golden Hills, Willoughby," said the saloon keeper. "Geoff Dawson is running things around here now. He's over in the mine office. Now he's wearin' clean clothes every single day. Man's gone 'citified on us."

Michael sent a shot of juice ten feet into the mud, cackling and coughing.

"Old Clem Dodd passed on, eh?" said Willoughby. "Well, I never did much care for Dawson, but if he's got our money, I guess I better learn to talk to the fool. Clean clothes? In this mud-hole?" He walked off, shaking his head and splashing mud with every step.

"He even wears a tie, Willoughby!" the old saloon keeper hollered out to him, giving off another loud cackle.

Willoughby opened the mine office door and saw Geoff Dawson standing behind the counter, wearing a suit, vest, white shirt, and string tie.

"So, you're runnin' things, now, hey Dawson?" said Willoughby. "Well, we got the supplies all distributed. I need to get the bills paid and my poke filled with some of your gold. We'll be gone at first light."

Willoughby was holding in a serious chuckle seeing Dawson in a clean suit of clothes. He even wore a watch fob and chain hanging from his vest pocket.

"Old Justin's Hole's becoming quite the metropolis, I see," remarked Willoughby, and part of that chuckle came to the surface.

"I've changed the pay schedule for the shipments," said Dawson. "You boys have been shorting us for years. I warned Clem about you thieving shysters. From now on, you'll get ten dollars each per load, and I'm going to do a full count on the goods before they are distributed."

"Ain't no way, Dawson. The rate is twelve-fifty for each pack mule, and if you even think of calling me a cheat again...I'll slice your liver for supper."

Willoughby was fingering the big Bowie knife he carried on his belt. Those who knew the mule skinner could recall more than one man who went six feet under from that blade. Willoughby stormed over to the door and motioned for Moose Nose and Ledgermain to come into the office. He also yelled out to the blacksmith.

"And bring that saloon keeper with you!"

The small mine office was jam-packed by the time everyone squeezed in.

"Dawson just told me that our rate for delivering all this good stuff has been cut from twelve-fifty for each pack mule to ten bucks," explained Willoughby angrily. "On top of that, he called me a thief. Now, I want you boys to know that I haven't shoved this knife of mine into his breast yet, but I better get this changed around pretty quick."

Geoff Dawson backed up behind the counter with an alarmed expression on his face.

"Sometimes this blade just does things on its own," exclaimed the mule skinner, "without any help from me."

He faked a lunge at the well-dressed chiseler behind the desk.

Everyone wore grim expressions.

"I ain't takin' a pay cut!" shouted Willoughby. "And neither are these fine skinners that work for me. If we don't get our pay and an apology right quick, this little village might not last through the night."

Before the echo of those words had settled, Moose Nose reached across the desk, grabbed Dawson by the neck, and dragged the man into the street. There, he slapped the suited merchant across the side of the head, letting the well-dressed fool go head-first into the wet muck. Moose Nose rubbed Dawson's face in the mud a couple of times and then jerked him to his feet. He marched him back into the office.

"Change your mind yet?" demanded Moose Nose, and then he slammed Dawson into a chair.

Nervous laughter bounced off the walls, but not from Dawson, Willoughby, Ledgermain, or Moose Nose. Dawson and Willoughby glared at each other. The mule skinner slowly drew his large gleaming knife from leather. Dawson's eyes grew bigger. He gripped the arms of the chair and everyone in the room held their breath and feared death. Jake Willoughby balanced the knife, his fingers curled around the carved handle, and he smiled ever so slowly. Dawson caved.

"All right," he howled. "Your pay will stay the same."

Willoughby's fingers remained curled around the beautifully carved knife handle. The mule skinner's anger increased and so did his smile, and he waited.

"And the apology, you big fool?" said Willoughby.

Dawson spit in defiance as the mule skinner reached out with his knife.

* * *

The whole village turned out that evening, all except one, of course, who was nursing a large cut across his left cheek, a cut that took fifteen stitches to close.

"Do you think he was sincere when he finally apologized?" Moose Nose asked, draining a tumbler of whiskey.

"He was sincere," Jake Willoughby answered, giving cute little Suzie another smile. "I thought it was a very sincere gesture to give us a little raise, as well."

The supply train left before sunrise, each mule carrying out the gold from the mine, as stated in the recently renewed contract.

# HORSE SENSE

His name is Jason P. Dougherty. His friends call him Tracker, and those who have looked down the barrel of his shotgun call him Sir.

"I'd even answer to 'Hey, there,' if the money was right," the bounty hunter was known to say.

Tracker was ten or so miles from the ranch; it was coming nightfall, and he was looking for someplace to throw his blanket when the sky lit up.

"Don't remember seeing anything like that," he muttered to himself as he watched a great fireball dance through low-lying clouds, showering flaming pieces in its trail and bouncing thunder off the rocky canyon walls. "Easy, now, Spot," he said to his paint cow horse, the one that was trying its best to flee this opening of Hade's gates, "Just a bolt of lightning."

Of course, Tracker knew it was more than that, and he watched as the fireball smashed into a mountain about three miles away.

"Come on, old boy, we got to find out what the heck that was. Sure didn't look like a lightning bolt. I don't think it was no kind of flying object I ever saw. This might just be something valuable. Sure could use some money right about now."

He got Spot halfway under control and jogged off up the trail toward what was now just a simmering little brush fire. It was soon to put itself out for lack of anything worthwhile to burn. The trail led into a canyon. Its rocky floor was shaped by millions of years of heavy snow, melting ice, avalanches, downed trees, falling boulders, and probably bones of the ancients.

"I got more than one deer in this area, and now, I'm gonna get something special. Wonder what that is. What do you think, Spot?"

The horse neighed and shook its head. The mount stepped cautiously forward. Through the years Tracker had spent hundreds of hours in the saddle, his horse being the only one to talk with. To the rider, Spot already answered in his own way. As they neared the little blaze, it was the aroma that set the stage for what was to come.

"That is one foul smell," Tracker grunted, stepping off his big paint. "Stand, old boy, stand still," he said, dropping the reins, knowing Spot wouldn't take more than two steps.

"Good fellow."

Pieces of something metallic and shiny were spread over about a hundred yards or so, the ground scorched black. Tracker stomped out the few little flares of fire and got near the wreckage.

"What on earth is this? Ain't never seen nothin' like it—ever. It's some kind of flying machine, that's for sure."

The main body of the craft was split open and badly charred.

"Dang me, but that's hot. Too bad it's gettin' dark. Better wait until tomorrow to look it over."

He walked back to his horse, stepped into the saddle, and trotted off in the direction of some nearby trees.

"Let's camp here, buddy," he said. He led Spot over to a wilted patch of grass, hobbled him, and spread his blanket. "Cold vittles tonight, pal."

Tracker pulled a piece of hard biscuit from his saddlebag and had supper. He laid down and wrapped the blanket around him. His dreams were filled with broken flying objects, visitors from Mars with ships bringing great vaults full of gold and emeralds. Those thoughts took him into deeper slumber.

* * *

It was the rustling of little rocks and gravel that brought Tracker straight up from a sound sleep, shotgun in hand.

"Don't move, now! Don't!" He leveled the gun at the intruder.

Tracker came to his feet, fully dressed, weapon shining bright in the morning sun. He looked into the eyes of what would never pass as another human being.

"Dang me, you smell bad, mister. Who are you?"

The creature stood about four feet tall and weighed a hefty two hundred pounds. He was wearing a slightly burned one-piece suit of silvery material, gloves of the same color, and brown boots that came about halfway up his short, fat legs. His arms, which were extraordinarily long, held a silver piece of metal about six inches in size.

"What are you?" Tracker asked, never lowering his shotgun.

In answer, he got noises and gibberish, and the stranger sat down all at once, letting the silver piece of metal slip from his hand. He was hurt, and Tracker could sense the being was in pain.

"Where in the heck are you from?"

Tracker's mind was overwhelmed, but he also knew he wasn't dreaming. He looked over at Spot, waiting for his reaction.

"What the blazes do you make of this, hoss?"

The strange being also looked at the horse and said something, or at least made some noises in that direction. Spot responded with a nicker and stood with head up staring at the creature. The strange being managed to move nearer and gently reached up and touched the man's shoulder, making a distressed sound.

"Hurt, eh?" said Tracker. "I got some liniment. Maybe that would help."

* * *

The average fella would get on his horse and flee the scene, getting his minutes of fame by telling anyone who would listen what happened. But old Tracker Dougherty was far and away, not average.

"Been here long?" he asked, slipping the lightweight silver coverall from the stranger's shoulder. "Oh, boy, do you stink! And that's a nasty bruise..."

The man rubbed some liniment on the creature's back as gently as he could, and the stranger grunted a couple of times. Tracker assumed he was saying thank you.

"Never been flying, myself. We don't have machines like yours. Always kind of skeered of the thought of not having my feet on the ground.

But it appears to me like you could use some more lessons yourself."

All this time, Spot had been working his way closer to where Tracker and the stranger were sitting. The stranger's face was different from that of a human's. Yes, there were two eyes, a nose and a mouth, and a couple of ears, but the way things were lined up, there appeared to be something wrong.

"You look more like a dog with a squashed-in face, or maybe a baboon, than a human. Of course, I've only seen pictures of them in books, you know. You feelin' better now?"

Tracker couldn't tell if the half-pint stranger felt better or not. Spot gave the slightest whinny, and the weird fellow stood up and walked to him. They put their heads together.

"Now, what on earth am I seeing?" Tracker said out loud. "My horse, terrified of butterflies, is nuzzling right up to this guy."

The man watched in amazement as an animated, silent conversation seemed to be taking place. The stranger walked back to where Tracker was standing, put one long arm out, six or seven fingers stretched, looking for a handshake.

"Well, dang me," the man said and took the proffered hand.

Tracker was jolted by a blast of energy that knocked him back about five feet. He sat in the rocks and dirt with a startled expression on his face. A beam of light appeared and the stranger walked into it and disappeared. More light ran across the wreckage and it vanished. In that brief contact, the entity gave Tracker answers to all of his questions.

Spot nickered softly, and the man got up, walked to his horse, removed the hobbles, and saddled him. He took one more look at the burned area on the mountainside and slipped into the saddle.

"I guess, from what that creature communicated, we'll be seeing more of them in the next few years, eh boy? Seemed like a nice guy. Dang me, though, his way of talking knocked me on my skinny rump."

Tracker snickered at that, and Spot neighed.

"I think we might have just met the original horse whisperer, old friend."

# AUTHOR BIO

Johnny Gunn, best-selling author, has written over forty-five novels, including the six-volume *Jack Slater* series. He is a member of two professional writing organizations: Western Fictioneers and Western Writers of America. After a successful career in journalism where he was the publisher and editor of the *Virginia City Legend*, Gunn now enjoys his retirement. He spends most of his time writing Western fiction, fly fishing on the Truckee River, horseback riding, and raising his own food. Gunn resides on his small hobby farm in Cold Springs, Nevada, with his wife, horses, dog, and various other animals.

# ILLUSTRATOR BIO

Illustrator Barabash Sviatoslav was born in the city of Kovel, Ukraine. At sixteen, he became interested in drawing. For fourteen years he continued his studies as an artist/painter. He attended and graduated from the Odessa Art College and the National Academy of Painting in Kyiv. Sviatoslav, a member of the Union of Artists, has participated in exhibitions of the Union of Artists of Ukraine and his own personal events.

Sviatoslav credits his grandfather, Alexander Manelyuk, a graphic designer, as being his first teacher. His grandfather taught him to appreciate the beauty of nature, especially landscapes with their endless varieties.

Among other art projects, Sviatoslav is currently illustrating books. Lately, he has become interested in digital art with its endless possibilities.

Dear Reader,

If you enjoyed reading *THE WEST: LAND OF OPPORTUNITY (A Collection),* please help promote the book by posting a review on Amazon.com and Goodreads.com and following Johnny Gunn on social media.

https://www.facebook.com/johnny.gunn.31
https://www.amazon.com/stores/author/B012BQB5X6#

You may also contact the author by writing to the following address:

Johnny Gunn
c/o Condor Publishing, Inc.
PO Box 39
Lincoln, Michigan 48742

Warm greetings from Condor Publishing, Inc.

www.ingramcontent.com/pod-product-compliance
Lightning Source LLC
Chambersburg PA
CBHW030411310726
48979CB00002B/371

* 9 7 8 1 9 3 1 0 7 9 6 4 8 *